Ambridge

An English Village Through The Ages

Six miles south of Borchester, nestling in a valley below Lakey Hill, is one of Borsetshire's most typical villages, Ambridge . . . This is a book about the land and its people, with sudden glimpses of the distant past through documents that have survived for hundreds of years, documents that contain names like Archer and Forrest, that are still well known in Ambridge today. There is also an astonishing collection of old photographs of rural life at the turn of the century, belonging to the Archer family, and twelve sketches of Ambridge today by local artist Caroline Bone . . .

It is the story of one small – but treasured – corner of England . . .

AMBRIDGE

AN ENGLISH VILLAGE THROUGH THE AGES

Jennifer Aldridge & John Tregorran

The Borchester Press
In association with Methuen

By arrangement with the British Broadcasting Corporation

A Methuen Paperback

AMBRIDGE
An English Village Through the Ages
ISBN 0 413 50170 1
First published in Great Britain 1981
by Eyre Methuen Ltd

This edition published 1982
by Methuen London Ltd.,
11 New Fetter Lane, London EC4P 4EE

Printed and bound in Great Britain by
William Clowes (Beccles) Limited, Beccles and London

Contents

Acknowledgements

This book could not have been compiled without the cooperation of the people of Ambridge itself: the villagers who supplied a rich fund of stories, sayings and traditions connected with the area, and the farmers who gave the landscape survey team every assistance in their work. The staff of Borchester Museum and the County Record Office at Felpersham were always patient and helpful. A special debt is owed to Dan Archer of Glebe Cottage, Ambridge, who supplied most of the early photographs used. The eighteenth-century wood engravings of country scenes by Thomas Bewick are from the collection of John and Carol Tregorran.

A number of people from outside the county have helped place this survey in its wider setting, and particular thanks are owed for information and illustrations to the Corinium Museum, Cirencester; Birmingham Central Library; the Shakespeare Birthplace Trust; Oxford Library; Mr J. Bond of the Oxfordshire Museums Service; and Mrs Joan Hunt of Rugby.

We would also like to take this opportunity to thank all those people in the world outside Borsetshire who cannot be named here, who helped make the whole concept possible.

J.A. and J.T.
Ambridge, 1981

Labourer and his scythe, crossing the footbridge over the River Am below Ambridge Court, 1888.

I

A Village of the Shires

Borsetshire is justly famed as the 'pastoral county', a land of quiet hills, slow-moving rivers and small villages: Penny Hassett, Waterley Cross, Loxley Barratt, Heybury, Little Croxley, Ambridge. This is the country Stanley Baldwin must surely have had in mind when he wrote of 'the sounds of England, the tinkle of the hammer on the anvil in the country smithy, the corncrake on a dewy morning, the sound of the scythe against the whetstone, and the sight of a plough team coming over the brow of a hill, the sight that has been seen in England since England was a land.'

The sight of the plough team is no more, the Ambridge smithy was converted into a garage in 1947 and the corncrake, like a hundred species of butterfly in Borsetshire alone, is gone for ever. Now, in the 1980s, the land itself is under attack, its hills and valleys, fields and lanes, ditches and hedgerows being changed more quickly and more completely than ever before.

The countryside has been called a living map, overwritten by generation after generation of farmers and builders, but still decipherable to the expert eye. The map is now in danger of being erased, not so much by motorways and urban developments, but by the deep plough and the hedge-grubbing machine. The five-acre fields with their ancient hedgerows, the meadows that have been mowed every year since Tudor times, the coverts and field ponds that provide a home for wildlife – all are disappearing, replaced by vast open acres where hay and corn can be grown and harvested more efficiently.

Concern for the landscape has grown rapidly in recent years, and in the autumn of 1979 Borsetshire County Council Department of Museum Services organized a series of lectures designed to help interested amateurs to study the changing landscape of their own parishes. The lectures were advertised in the *Borchester Echo* as part of Borchester Technical College's usual programme of evening classes, and attracted the attention of two Ambridge residents, Jennifer Aldridge of Home Farm and John Tregorran of Manor Court. Jennifer was already playing a prominent role in the local conservation move-

Ambridge church at dusk, photographed from the water meadows of the River Am.

ment and John had spent many years compiling material for a history of Ambridge. They were later joined by Shula and Pat Archer, Freddie Danby and Caroline Bone.

The course of lectures started in September and ended two months later, in good time for the participants to make a start on their survey work in the winter months. Seven parishes in the Borchester area have since been mapped, but the Ambridge survey is the only one so far to be published, and its appearance is due in no small measure to the sympathy and encouragement of Jack Woolley, owner of the Grey Gables Country Club and a director of the Borchester Press.

It was Mr Woolley who realized the potential interest, among a wide readership, of a book which would chart in detail the landscape history of a typical village of the English Shires. His also was the suggestion that the Ambridge team broaden the scope of their work and include the 'human history' of the village, its traditions, folk-saying and people. Much of this material is the result of oral evidence collected over the years by John Tregorran.

The degeneration of the national 'folk memory' is not a subject that can be elaborated on here, but it is certainly true that for whatever cause – the growth of literacy, the ease of travel, the influence of radio and television – there has been a weakening of local ties and a loss of local traditions. John Tregorran has spoken to many of the older inhabitants of Ambridge and its surrounding villages and collected a rich store of folk memories that would otherwise have been lost entirely. Weather lore, sayings and superstitions, rural customs and traditional celebrations, farming methods before the age of the tractor, the way people

'The steep bank where the willows grow'; looking down on Grange Farm.

lived and the food they ate before electricity, mechanization and the motor car changed rural England for ever – John Tregorran has captured on tape the last breath of country life as it existed for a thousand years.

What follows, then, is firstly the results of the landscape survey itself, carried out over eighteen laborious months. (Let nobody think it is easy! An entire day plodding round the slopes of Lakey Hill or squelching along the muddy banks of the Am in February might yield only a couple of tentative lines on a sketch map.) The survey covers the landscape history of the village up to the eighteenth century, and includes the identification of the site of Ambridge's deserted medieval village and the discovery of a traceried medieval window in a barn at Grange Farm. The team's efforts to establish the Saxon boundaries of Ambridge and the dates of the principal woods and boundary hedges make it possible to say, with reasonable confidence, which features of the man-made landscape have survived for the past nine hundred years.

The folk-lore of Ambridge is based on John Tregorran's research, supplemented by information collected by the survey team. Traditional Ambridge food and recipes were investigated by Shula Archer and Caroline Bone, and it was Caroline, a local artist, who did the twelve sketches of Ambridge for this book.

There is also a section devoted entirely to a rare and fascinating collection of old photographs, many of them taken in the second half of the nineteenth century. They include pictures of specific occasions, like the Ambridge Sunday School outing of 1910, and also some of the best photographs of farming just after the First World War so far discovered. There are also early photographs from the family album of one particular Ambridge family – the Archers of Brookfield Farm.

Apart from a dozen or so photographs kindly loaned by individuals, all the photographs were for many years in the possession of Doris Archer, and when, sadly, she died in October 1980 her husband Dan willingly loaned them to his granddaughter Shula for inclusion in an exhibition at Home Farm, and generously gave permission for their inclusion in this book.

The River Am.

2

Before the Ice

For anyone interested in exploring the landscape of Ambridge, the obvious first step is to drive out of the village along the Felpersham road, turn left along the small lane signposted 'Hollowtree' and stop after about a mile at the point where an unmetalled track leads up to Willow Farm. Here a county council signpost points to a public footpath which leads, after about thirty-five minutes of brisk walking, to the summit of Lakey Hill.

From here, looking south over the brambles and yellow-flowering gorse, the whole of the parish can be seen, with its farms, woodlands and its meandering, slow-moving river. The historian Maitland described England's ordnance survey maps as a 'marvellous palimpsest', but to anyone looking out over the Am valley, the land itself appears as a palimpsest on which man's activities have been recorded, erased and then inscribed again. Man has occupied England for only a short time, but he has succeeded in changing and modifying almost all environments. The valley of the Am is no exception.

To the east the pastures of Willow Farm slope down to the river, then the land rises to the dense woodland of Long Wood and Leader's Wood – the last remains of the once extensive Forest of Am. South of the woodland, across the ploughed fields, is the red tiled roof of Home Farm and the metallic gleam of its clustering dutch barns. From its concrete and macadamed yards and driveway modern tractors emerge to work the 1,500 acres of productive land that have been won from the forest during the past five hundred years.

Closer, with gardens running down to the river, is Ambridge Hall – a mid-Victorian villa that must have been a monstrous eyesore when it was built (as a doctor's house, by the enlightened squire of the day, Mr James Lawson-Hope) but which has now acquired a certain charm, with its weatherbeaten brickwork and roof of dull green tiles.

Leaving Ambridge Hall the river bends to the south through the fertile valley floor, passing what used to be, only forty years ago, five small, self-contained working farms: Sawyers, Hollowtree, Brookfield, Wynfords and Bull Farm. Now only Brookfield, with its late

Ambridge and the Vale of Am, looking south east from Lakey Hill.

Harebells on Lakey Hill.

The Vale of Am from Lakey Hill; an eighteenth-century engraving. 'Borsetshire can proudly call itself the pastoral county, beloved by the lyric poets of the eighteenth century and immortalized by the painters of the classic English school. Its western hills are noted sheep country (although the ancient blue-back Hassett sheep survives now only in the Darrington Rare Breeds Centre) and the Vale of Borset is a country of mixed farms, rich pastures and small villages.' *Borsetshire Guide*, 1980.

seventeenth-century black-and-white farmhouse, remains in its own right. The others have been absorbed into larger units and many hedges and boundaries have disappeared.

Looking to the south east, across the valley over the main Felpersham road, the land is seen to rise gently to Ten Elms Rise (they are all dead and apart from the stumps of two trees the wood has long since been cut and burned) and directly to the south is Heydon Berrow, once common land belonging to the people of several neighbouring parishes, but long since 'purchased' by the Ambridge estate.

From this high view the village itself appears small, tidy and well contained – the Borsetshire County Structure Plan allows no development at Ambridge other than a limited amount of 'in-filling'. The reason for the original settlement here is instantly apparent, for the village lies at the point where the valley track from Hollerton in the south at one time converged with the pack-road over the hills from Borchester.

Beyond the village the land rises yet again, country park and golf course merging into the slopes of Blossom Hill. In summer the gothic pile of Grey Gables Country Club is mercifully hidden behind its screen of magnificent horse-chestnuts, but when the summer air is still and heavy, the distant murmur of the A1999 can occasionally be heard.

And so back to Lakey Hill itself, with its gently-sloping turf enriched for centuries by 'the golden hoof', its brambles and broom, its splendid if unspectacular views over the English countryside. On the very summit is a small patch of dark soil that is never fully colonized by the surrounding turf, and which bears witness to the other history of Ambridge: the history of its people. 'From Clee to Heaven the beacons burn,' wrote A.E. Housman, and Lakey Hill has for centuries been part of the same chain, its bonfire joining Clee and Malvern to the

Cotswolds, Edge Hill and the beacons of the south, swiftly passing news of national victory or approaching danger.

One of Ambridge's oldest residents, Dan Archer of Glebe Cottage, remembers when, as a young man of twenty-two, he was put in charge of building the 1918 victory bonfire – and how his mother claimed it was a 'poor thing' compared to the bonfire his father built on Lakey Hill to celebrate Queen Victoria's Jubilee in 1887. Mr Archer's son, Phil, has vivid memories of the beacon that was lit on the eve of the Queen's coronation, and his daughter Shula was on the committee which organized the Jubilee bonfire in 1977.

That bonfire is now part of the history of Lakey Hill – a history that stretches back to the time man first entered the Am valley; that stretches back, if our conceit will allow us to admit it, for thousands of centuries before then.

On the ridge of the Malvern Hills and the western slope of Borsetshire's Hassett Hills are outcrops of pre-Cambrian rock, the oldest and hardest on earth. In the unimaginable past these heights stood forth as islands in the Silurian sea, which laid down round its shores the quartzite of the Lickeys and the limestones of Churcham. Later the whole of Borsetshire was a vast lake, its stagnant waters loaded with salt and lime, which when evaporated gave rise to the rock-salt and gypsum deposits of Felpersham. Then the sea crept in again from the south, turning the salt lake into a sea so deep and vast that even the Malverns and Hassett Hills were submerged. In these waters were deposited the blue limestones and clays of the lower Avon Valley, the yellow oolite of Churcham and Lakey Hill, and finally a layer of white chalk.

The Ice Ages came and the chalk was washed away. At Child's Farm, Loxley Barratt, there is a quarry face considered important enough to have been conserved at the request of the Borsetshire branch of the Trust for Nature Conservation. The quarry shows the red clay of Borsetshire's Keuper marl and over it a topsoil of sandy gravel, a drift laid down a quarter of a million years ago at the place where two enormous glaciers met.

Borsetshire has been described, with good reason, as 'the cockpit of England'. Romans and Cornovii, Saxons and Danes, they fought through the centuries for possession of its fertile soil. After them came Lancastrians and Yorkists, Roundheads and Cavaliers, with their epic and bloody battles on the Borsetshire plain. But no confrontation, no clash of brute force, can have been greater than that first mighty struggle over 250,000 years ago, when one glacier pushing east from North Wales brought with it volcanic rocks and limestone, and the other forced its way west laden with chalk and flints.

They met along a line through what was to become, thousands of years later, the Forest of Arden, then down through the village of Claverdon in Warwickshire and across to Churcham, Ambridge, Netherbourne and down the valley of the Am to Felpersham. Along

Lakey Hill. Looking down Cow Ridge towards Penny Hassett.

this line the Welsh glacier deposited huge, isolated rocks which later became known as 'warstones' or 'hoarstones' in places where they marked man-made boundaries. (The Arenig boulder in Cannon Hill Park, Birmingham, the warstone in Warstone Lane Cemetery, Hockley, and the Devil's Stone at Darrington are well known examples. In the Ambridge area, the hoarstone marking the Saxon boundary with Penny Hassett is of a very modest size.)

The ice retreated. To the west the Severn was diverted from its original course into the Dee, and bent southwards to the Bristol Channel. The Am and the Borsetshire Avon assumed their present paths through the dense forests and the marshes left by the last salt tides. Borsetshire was now something like its present geographical shape, and in time came animal life – ichthyosaurus, mammoth, hippopotamus and reindeer bones have been found in the county – and finally there came man himself.

3

Prehistoric Ambridge

We know, to some extent, the history of prehistoric Ambridge through the history of Borsetshire and its surrounding counties. The human tribes left in Britain after the submergence of the English Channel (Palaeolithic or Old Stone Age man) lived mainly south of a line joining the Bristol Channel and the Wash, and it was not until 1920 that a number of Old Stone Age pick-axe handles were found near Worcester, and other finds were made which established the presence of Palaeolithic man in north Borset.

After the Old Stone Age, Britain was invaded by three successive races – Iberians, Goidels, and Brythons – more commonly known as Neolithic, Bronze and Iron Age man.

The Iberians were still of the Stone Age, but their implements were smoothed and ground instead of being chipped. They were mainly herdsmen who settled on the hills and made little attempt at extensive cultivation. They were followed, in about one thousand BC, by the Goidels from Central Europe who introduced bronze weapons and implements. The Goidels occupied Borsetshire for some four hundred years and finds of Bronze Age weapons have been made in numerous places, particularly in valleys where rivers were fordable. The Goidels cremated their dead and an urn containing charred bones – presumably the remains of a chieftain – was found on the summit of Hassett Hill in 1884.

It was in about 600 BC that men of the Iron Age – the Britons – arrived and drove the Goidels, like the Iberians before them, west into Wales. The Britons had superior weapons, personal adornments and the beginnings of an art. The Borchester Torc, now in the British Museum, was found by a farm labourer in 1886 and, like the Perdiswell Torc from Worcester, consists of twenty small pieces of bronze, twisted and tooled and mounted on an iron wire. Iron Age barrows exist at three sites in the county and there is evidence of a major British camp by Hassett Bridge that has still to be excavated.

In the century before the Romans, east Borsetshire was the meeting place of three British tribes, the Cornovii based on Shropshire, the

North of the Ambridge parish boundary, the walls of the Iron Age hillfort on Hassett Hill are still standing under a layer of turf. A preliminary excavation in 1972 showed evidence of British occupation after the withdrawal of Roman forces from England.

Coritani from Leicestershire and the Iceni from the South East. Borsetshire appears to have been well populated by the standards of the times, but in today's terms it would have seemed empty and untouched. Such things are difficult to measure, but it seems likely that there are at least two hundred times as many people living in the county now than there were in 100 BC.

In many parts of the Midlands prehistoric occupation has left few marks on the landscape and evidence of man's activity is hard to find. At one time it was thought that this was due to the late survival of the primeval forest over what was to become the Midland Shires, but in recent years evidence has accumulated which suggests that the landscape was intensively exploited well before 2000 BC and that settlement was much denser and cultivation much more widespread than had once been thought. The reason why so little is obvious today is that later cultivation has to a large extent obliterated the traces.

Only on the higher ground, where ploughing has until recently been more intermittent, do any recognizable prehistoric monuments survive. On Lakey Hill a group of three barrows or burial mounds of Bronze Age date can still be seen, although these have been much reduced by ploughing since the Second World War, and are now about a metre high. These features lie on the parish boundary and can be identified with the 'three *lows*' recorded on the Saxon boundary charter for Ambridge, to be discussed in chapter six.

On the lower ground – the Vale of Am; the valley now containing Ambridge Hall, Willow Farm and Home Farm; the pasture of Brookfield; and the village itself – evidence of prehistoric man's activities is confined to chance finds. A Neolithic stone axe was found in the grounds of Ambridge Hall in 1893 and is now in Borchester Museum. A single stray find of this sort, however, means relatively little in terms of occupation on the site. Only where there are considerable concentrations of finds is it likely that some sort of settlement is represented – and in Ambridge the survey team found quantities of flint fragments in a ploughed field on the slope overlooking the Am River

Trees on the summit of Lakey Hill near the three Bronze Age barrows mentioned in the Saxon charter.

below the Hollowtree Pig Unit. Flint occurs only in chalk or in glacial deposits derived from chalk, and does not occur naturally in the Ambridge area, so the flint fragments had clearly been brought in from elsewhere. Expert help from Borsetshire Museum Services showed – through a detailed examination of the flints – that the site must have been occupied and reoccupied intermittently over a long period of time, its main attraction perhaps being the spring of fresh water which rises at the upper end of the present field and drains down to the river.

The field is currently known as 'Long Ground' but in 1839 the Tythe Commissioners recorded its name as being 'Hobbs Hole' and there is a local superstition to the effect that the devil drinks from the spring (a pump was provided in the late 1890s) every Saturday night on his way home from the Cat and Fiddle public house. This is relevant only in that sites of former occupation frequently gather round them traditions involving the supernatural.

Amongst the considerable quantity of waste flakes and cores found by the survey team were a few more distinctive implements, including some half-dozen microliths (the tiny flint blades used by Mesolithic peoples around 7000–5000 BC when Ambridge was still under extensive forest cover); a variety of scrapers and borers, and a couple of leaf-shaped arrowheads of Neolithic date (c 3000–2000 BC), by which time there had been considerable clearance for cultivation; and several barbed and tangled arrowheads typical of the Bronze Age (c 1000 BC), when the landscape was fully organized and relatively heavily populated. This sort of assemblage is typical of many sites in Borsetshire and the Midlands in general.

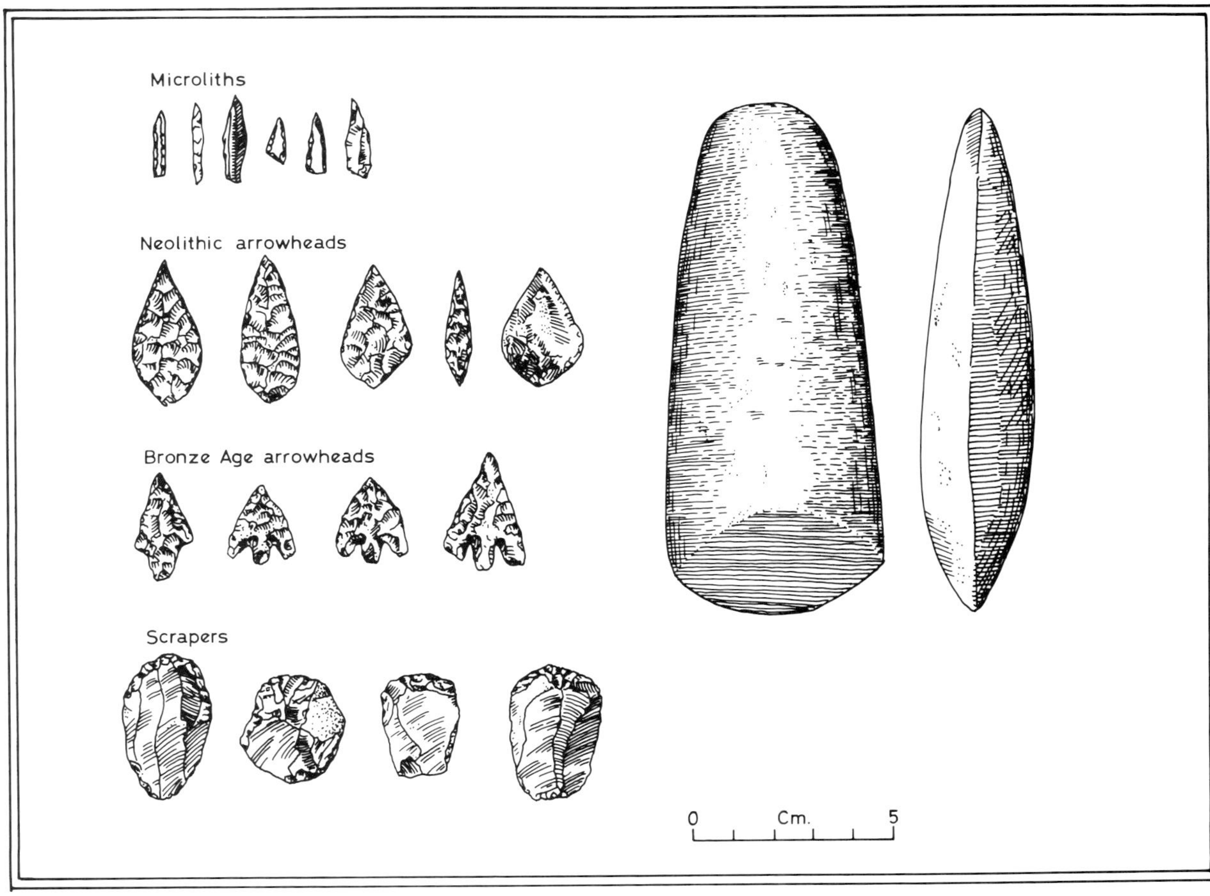

Prehistoric finds. Right, Neolithic Stone Age axe from the grounds of Ambridge Hall; left, flints from the field below Hollowtree Pig Unit.

It is more difficult to find much evidence of Iron Age occupation in Ambridge, though it is inherently likely that intensive settlement and cultivation continued. Several eighteenth- and nineteenth-century historians believed that they could detect evidence of earthworks to the south east of Heydon Berrow and thought that these were the remains of an Iron Age hill fort similar to the one on Hassett Hill; but recent re-examination has shown that these earthworks are lynchets or cultivation terraces, which represent the highest extent of medieval openfield strip cultivation, the more typical expression of which is the ridge and furrow, to be discussed in chapter eight. Although pottery was widely used, its friable nature means that it tends not to survive continued ploughing and weathering, and there is much less chance of locating Iron Age sites from pottery scatters than the Roman sites.

The most likely prospect for further discovery of prehistoric sites in the area is now through aerial photography, but this can only be achieved over a period of many years. The clay, marl and limestone

Pumping water from a spring at Hollowtree, 1901. The field was later identified as the site of a prehistoric settlement.

soils of the parish are less responsive to the processes which reveal ploughed-out ancient sites from the air than are, for example, the gravels of the Avon, Severn and Thames Valleys, and the conditions which favour the discovery of new sites through aerial photography occur more rarely.

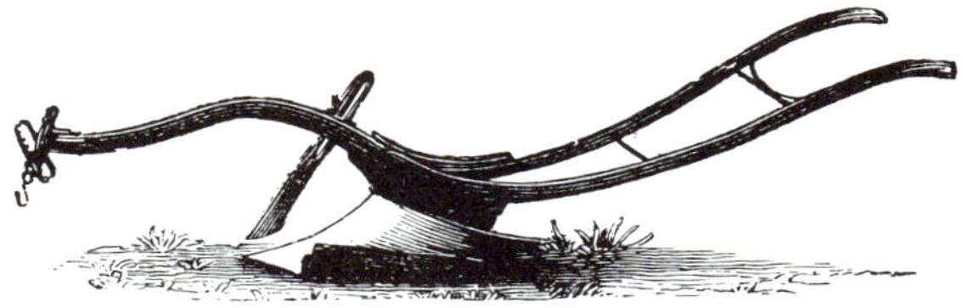

4

Roman Ambridge

Archaeologists have come to realize in recent years that the population of Britain during the four centuries of Roman administration was much greater than was once thought. In many parts of the country, including Borsetshire, any single parish might now be expected to contain at least four or five settlements of Roman date.

One way in which it is possible to detect prehistoric and Romano-British settlements which have left little surface trace through later ploughing is from the evidence of crop marks, sometimes visible from ground level, though usually best seen and photographed from the air. A ditch or a pit dug into the subsoil will never be restored to the nature of the undisturbed ground around it, even centuries after it has been filled up and the ground surface levelled off. The filling of such a feature is likely to hold more moisture and to have a higher humus content than the surrounding ground, and this will produce an effect on the growth of any crop planted over it. As the crop changes colour during ripening, from green to yellow and later from yellow to brown, this process may be delayed for a week or more over places where its roots encounter the damper soil of the archaeological features. The pattern of the buried ditches and pits will therefore be picked out in plan as a strong colour difference in the crop at certain times of year. The shape and arrangement of the features revealed will often suggest what date and what sort of site is present: circular marks, for example, are often the perimeter ditches of ploughed-out Bronze Age round barrows, while Romano-British farmsteads often appear as rather larger square or rectangular enclosures. The richer humus content of the buried features and the fact that the crop roots can penetrate deeper into the subsoil also tends to give rise to a more vigorous crop growth over them, and the plan of the site may sometimes be revealed through the difference in crop height rather than as a colour difference.

Another way of identifying early sites is by walking the fields when there is no crop after ploughing. Long-continued human occupation on a site will often result in a darkening of the soil there, because of the local build-up of organic material. Such areas were often recognized by

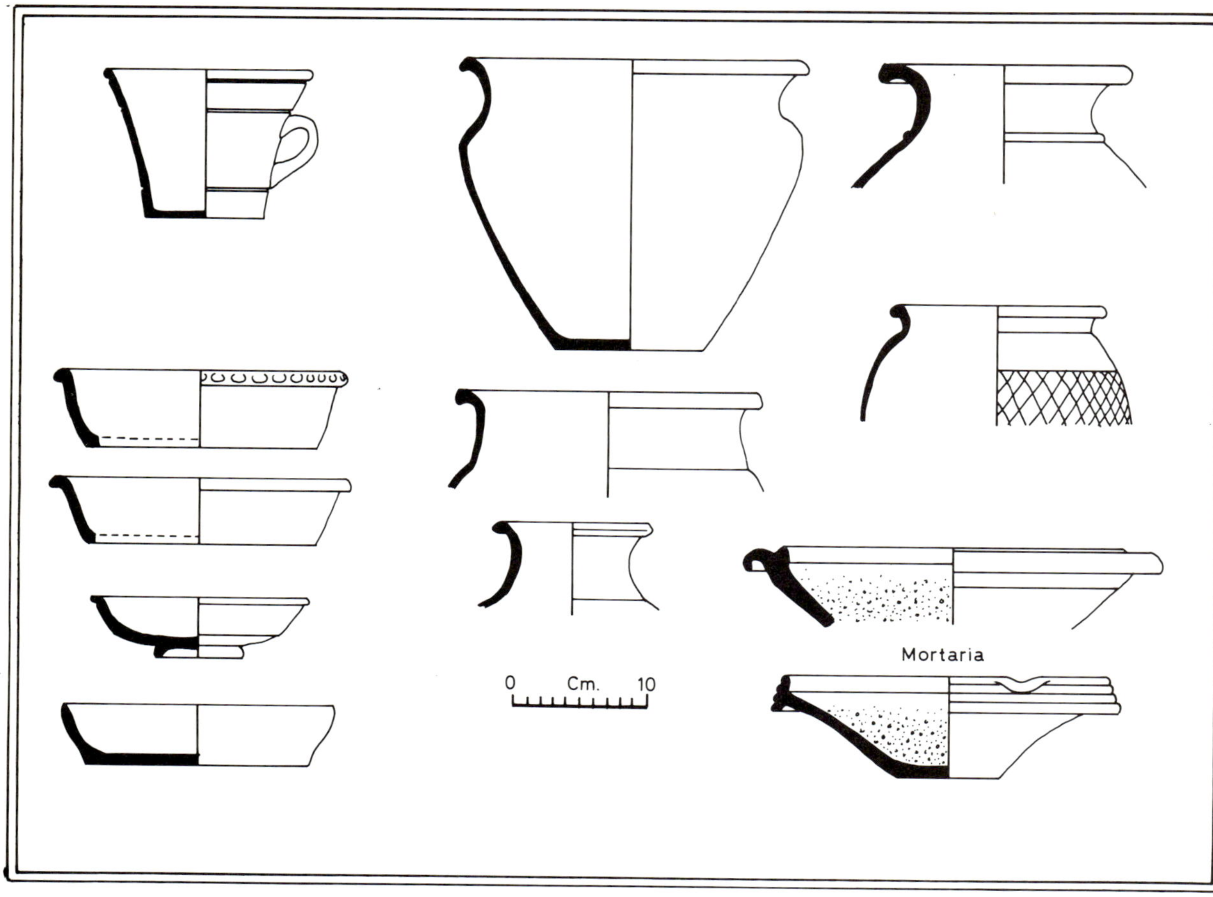

Romano-British coarse pottery found at Jiggin's Field.

later generations of farmers, and given distinctive field-names, such as 'Blacklands'. Fields with names of this type will often produce scatters of pottery and building materials under the plough, even where there is no crop-mark evidence. Romano-British sites in particular tend to produce considerable quantities of pottery, because pottery was widely used and was of sufficiently high quality to survive in the soil, whereas earlier pottery has often failed to survive through weathering and erosion. When such a site is discovered, it should not be disturbed by the random collection of the larger or more interesting looking pieces of pottery seen on the surface, but should instead be reported to the local museum. The detailed survey of such a site requires some care and knowledge, involving the marking-out of the field with poles and tapes into a ten or twenty metre grid, and the systematic collection and mapping of all the surface finds. This will often allow the main buildings to be located and sometimes their functions to be identified, and will reveal whether the whole site is entirely of one period or whether different parts have been occupied at different dates.

Summer at Home Farm with poppies, corn and camomile.

It was around AD 46, some three years after the Roman invasion of Britain under Emperor Claudius, that the XIVth Legion crossed the line of what was to become the Fosse Way, overrunning without difficulty the native tribes of Borsetshire. From then until the early fifth century, the county was a settled and prosperous part of the Roman Empire.

The administration of the area was based on the tribal capital of the Dubunni at Cirencester (Corinium) but Borchester was an important trading post, lying as it did to the west of the rich corn lands of the

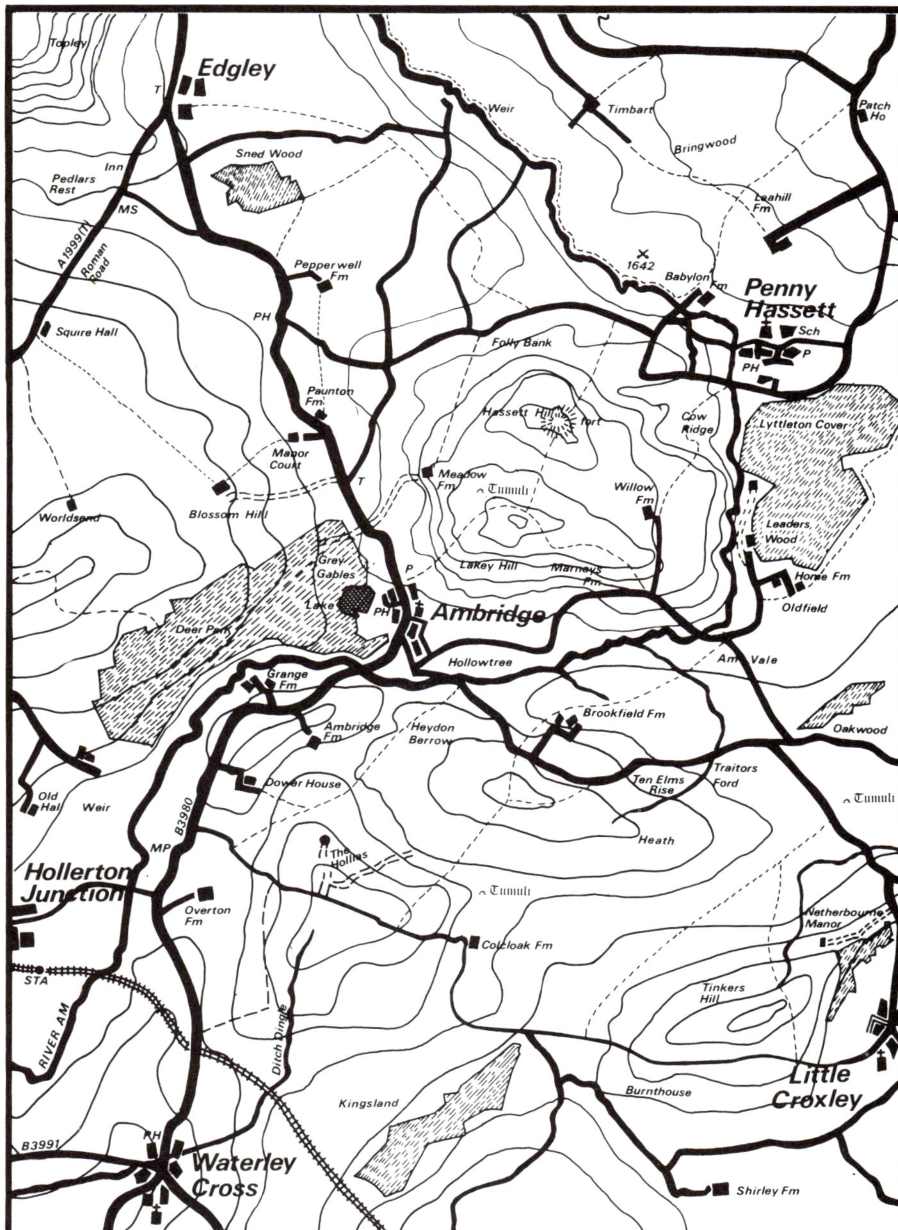

Ambridge and its neighbouring villages.

Borsetshire plain. A major Roman road (now the A1999) ran north through Borchester from Akeman Street to Droitwich.

As far as Ambridge is concerned, the relatively unresponsive nature of the soils to air photography has meant that the main chance of locating sites in the parish has been through field walking.

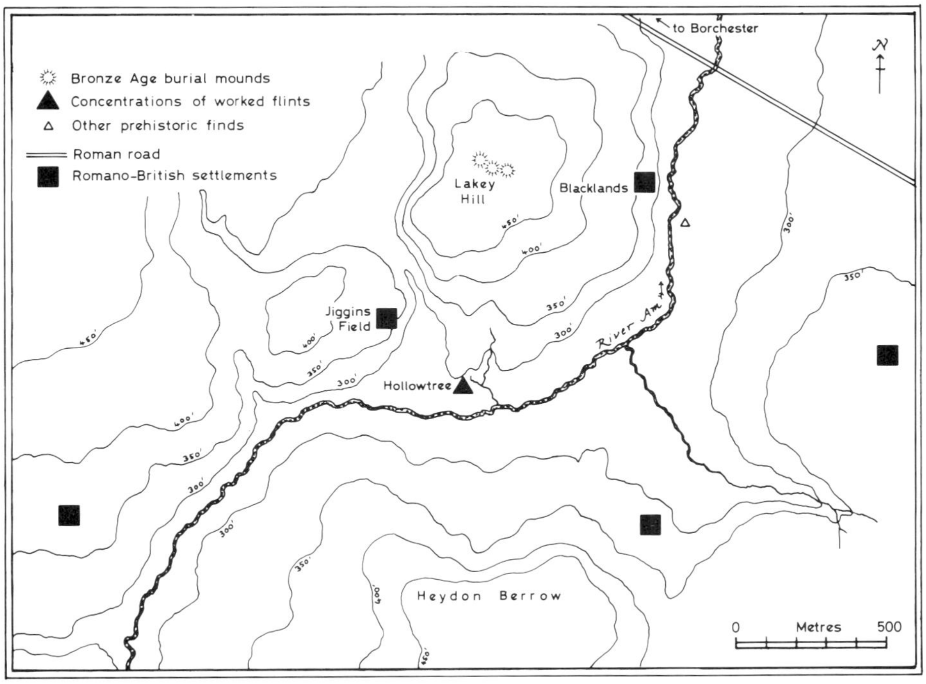

Prehistoric and Romano-British Ambridge.

One Romano-British site at Jiggin's Field has been known since the accidental discovery of quantities of pottery there during the cutting of a new drainage ditch in the 1880s. This site was partly excavated in 1975–6 due to the threat of deep ploughing. The excavation report of this site is published in full in the county archaeological journal, the *Transactions of the Borsetshire Archaeological Society,* Vol LXVIII. The site was a farmstead comprising several ranges of timber buildings including both domestic accommodation and agricultural ranges, within a ditched rectangular enclosure, occupied from the second to the late fourth century AD.

Finds of Romano-British material during field-walking by the survey team have indicated that several other, similar settlements existed within or near the bounds of the present parish. (The most definite locations are the south-east corner of 'Great Ground', Home Farm, and 'Pound Close' at Sawyers Farm.) The concentrations of pottery and other finds on each site have been carefully mapped and the details sent in to the County Museum to be filed with the County Sites and Monuments Record housed there. Pottery has been by far the commonest material discovered, and the bulk of this comprises locally-made buff, brown, grey and black coarse wares, including cooking-pots, bowls, dishes, and jugs. Fragments of mortaria, with gritted surfaces used for the pounding of food in preparation, were brought in from other parts of the Midlands. The finer-quality pottery, such as the distinctive glossy hard red samian ware imported from the continent and the decorated wares made in specialized centres elsewhere in Britain, were poorly represented. Very little metal-work has been found on any of the sites, apart from occasional bronze coins which have been collected over a number of years by gamekeeper Tom Forrest, and which remain in his possession (the find-spot of each coin having been carefully recorded and the details lodged with the County Museum). No tesserae were found to suggest the existence of mosaic pavements, and no fragments of roof or flue tiles were found. The evidence indicates that the Romano-British settlements in Ambridge were small farmsteads with timber buildings.

The distribution of Roman sites is almost certainly incomplete, as it has not been possible to examine every field in the parish under ideal conditions. The field called Blacklands at Willow Farm might have been expected to yield a site from the evidence of the field name and did produce several dozen abraded potsherds (though only on the second survey attempt – the first survey was carried out under poor weather conditions before the survey team had properly mastered the techniquest of grid-survey work). The quantity of potsherds was not sufficient to suggest that a settlement lay beneath the field itself; but the fact that the finds of pottery were concentrated along the eastern edge of the field suggests that the centre of a possible site might lie beneath the adjacent paddock which was under grass and therefore produced no finds.

5

Ham, Ley, Ton and Berrow

Place-names can be a very useful type of evidence for the landscape historian, but their modern form can sometimes be very misleading. It is always necessary to trace the present names back to their earliest recorded form, which for many villages will occur either in a Saxon charter or in the Domesday Book. Their interpretation is a task for the specialist, and place-name scholars have themselves drastically revised many of their earlier theories in recent years.

The sort of difficulties which may be encountered is exemplified by the common place-name ending *-ham,* which occurs in Felpersham. The first part of this name is probably derived from the name of one of

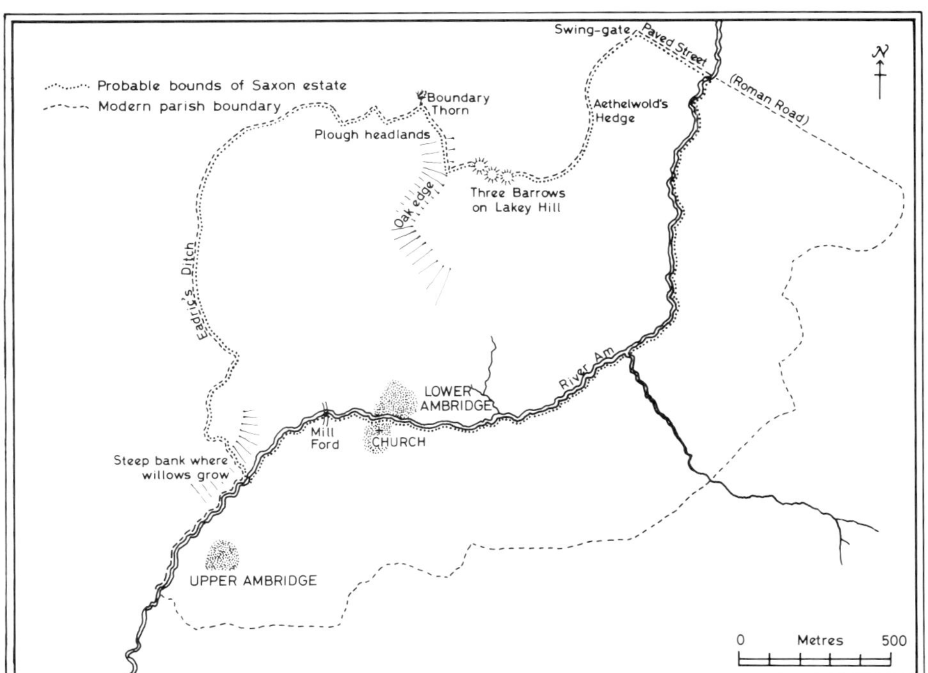

Anglo-Saxon Ambridge.

its early settlers or landowners. The second part may, however, be derived from one of two quite different Anglo-Saxon words: *hām,* meaning a village, or *hamm,* meaning a riverside meadow or a promontory within a river-meander or marsh from which a village may subsequently have taken its own name.

Other common place-name elements are more straightforward. Netherbourne comes from the Anglo-Saxon for lower stream. Names ending in *-ton,* such as Hollerton or Leyton Cross, are usually derived from the Anglo-Saxon *tun,* meaning a farm or estate in open country. This contrasts with the equally common type of name ending in *-ley,* such as Waterley Cross or Edgeley, which are derived from the Anglo-Saxon word *leah,* meaning a woodland clearing. The distribution of names of this sort can be used as a guide to which areas were largely under cultivation and which areas still retained considerable woodland cover in the Anglo-Saxon period.

Ambridge is a difficult case, because it takes its name from a feature which appeared in the landscape at a relatively late date, the bridge over the River Am. The original name of the village may have been quite different, and the importance of the new crossing over the river at this point may have led to the change.

Some names are tautologous, repeating their own meaning, perhaps because the significance of part of the name had been forgotten in the distant past. For example, Heydon Berrow is likely to include two Anglo-Saxon words, *dun* and *beorg,* both meaning a hill.

Less widespread than names ending in *-ham, -ton* or *-ley,* but nonetheless still quite common, are names ending in *-chester* or *-castor,* of which Borchester is the main local example. Such places indicate the sites of Roman towns, forts or other settlements.

One further interesting name is Penny Hassett. The first part of the name looks like a tautologous hybrid of Anglo-Saxon and British words: the British or Welsh *penn,* meaning a headland, promontory or hill, and the Anglo-Saxon *eg,* meaning an island or sometimes a hill rising above and surrounded by lower ground. The second part of the name is derived from the early medieval lords of the manor, the Hassetts – there are many similar examples of landowners' names being attached to distinguish places, particularly where there is more than one village of the same name close by.

6

Athelstan's Charter

From the end of the seventh century to the Norman Conquest, gifts of land, granted by the king to one of his subjects, were usually recorded by charters. The texts of many of these documents have survived, although often only in the form of later copies. In some cases the copies were made not long after the original, and reproduce faithfully the content of the first charter; in other cases the charters are clearly forgeries, drawn up at a later date by monastic or other landlords trying to claim a block of land where their title was questionable.

At this early period maps were unknown. The only way a block of land could be identified was by describing a perambulation around its boundaries, listing significant landmarks such as streams, ridges of high ground, plough headlands, prehistoric barrows, or prominent trees, in the order in which they were encountered.

Not all of the features recorded in a charter are likely to survive in the landscape today, but it is often possible to identify enough of the boundary landmarks to be able to reconstruct the bounds of the Saxon land grant with a fair degree of accuracy – particularly in cases where part or all of the estate has survived in the form of a modern parish.

There is a charter covering the grant of an estate of 6 *cassati* or 'hides' of land in Ambridge in 936 to the wealthy monastery of St Mary in Worcester. The land was granted by Athelstan, third of the great West Saxon kings, and in return the monks were requested to pray for an English victory over the Celtic, Danish and Norwegian forces massing in Northern Britain. (The following year the monks' prayers were answered when Athelstan defeated Constantine, King of the Scots, and Olaf of Dublin at the battle of Brunanburh.) The Ambridge charter survives only in the form of a later copy, but the internal evidence within the text suggests that it reproduces the substance of a genuine grant and is not a total forgery.

The bounds of the estate are described in the Anglo-Saxon language, translated as follows. The identity of some of the landmarks along the boundary is unambiguous, such as the River Am, and other landmarks can be located from field-work with a reasonable degree of certainty;

Willows still grow alongside the River Am north of Grange Farm at the point where Eadric's Ditch begins.

but, as with many such documents, there are problems in attempting to reconstruct the whole circuit. Some of the features which require comment are described further below. The actual land-grant reads:

'First from the Mill Ford (1) along the Am as far downstream as the steep bank where the willows grow, then along Eadric's Ditch (2) to Tanescoec (3), then along the plough headlands (4) to the boundary thorn, from the boundary thorn to the top of the oak edge, then over the three lows (5), then along Aethelwold's Hedge (6) to the swing-gate, then along the paved street (7) to the Am and so back to the mill ford.'

(1) The Mill Ford was probably the main crossing over the River Am before the building of the bridge which gave the place its name. Water-mills were beginning to appear in some quantity in England during the course of the tenth century, and are not infrequently recorded in charter bounds.

(2) Eadric's Ditch is almost certainly to be identified with the large bank and ditch now followed by the present parish boundary along the western side of the country park. The bank has been broken down along many stretches, and is hardly discernible for much of its course. It is most clearly in evidence where the ditch itself has been widened to form a cart track used by estate workers. The hedge running alongside the bank has been severely mutilated by modern hedge-trimming machinery, but nevertheless remains one of the oldest hedgerows in Ambridge.

(3) Tanescoec is the name of a landmark which can neither be translated nor accurately located on the ground. There are some difficulties in following the boundaries of the estate onwards from this point, as several of the listed features have not survived or are insufficiently distinctive to be located with any degree of certainty.

(4) The plough headlands may be represented by a stretch of the parish boundary describing a somewhat zig-zag course north of Grey Gables. A series of open-field furlongs is still visible here as ridge and furrow, and the boundary has clearly been drawn round their headlands.

(5) The three lows must be the three Bronze Age barrows still faintly visible on top of Lakey Hill. Prehistoric monuments were often used in this way as landmarks on the bounds of charter grants. The modern form 'low' is from the Anglo-Saxon word *hlaw,* meaning hill, mound or barrow, and often occurs in field-names such as Low Hill.

Eadric's Ditch, now a cart track used by estate workers.

(6) Aethelwold's Hedge is almost certainly to be identified with a long, gently-curving stretch of hedge followed by the present parish boundary around the north-west side of Willow Farm, rich in hedgerow species. Both Aethelwold and Eadric were presumably the owners of neighbouring estates, though they are unknown from other historical sources.

(7) The paved street is almost certainly the Roman road from Loxley Barratt to Borchester which survives only as a cart track. It forms part of the parish boundary in the north east.

Much of the above description is still uncertain – landscape features have changed and there are puzzling illogicalities when the Saxon boundary is set against a modern map of Ambridge. But it is clear that the estate granted in 936 was smaller than the present parish, and consisted only of that part north of the River Am, excluding Grange Farm, which formed a separate estate of four hides. The two estates were temporarily in the hands of the same landowner at the time of the Domesday survey, but were later separated again. Grange Farm and the separate estate of Upper Ambridge will be discussed further in chapter ten.

The plough headlands, north of Grey Gables, looking down on the country park.

7

Domesday Ambridge

Twenty years after the Norman Conquest, when William the Conqueror was securely established on the English throne, he ordered a vast and detailed survey of his kingdom in order to assess its value for taxation. The result was the Domesday Book, the Book of Judgement from which there was no appeal. It was a remarkably accurate and detailed ledger of the country's wealth. 'So very narrowly he (the King) caused it to be traced out', says the *Anglo-Saxon Chronicle,* 'that there was not one single hide, nor one yard of land, nor even – it is shame to tell, though it seemed to him no shame to do – an ox, nor a cow, nor a swine, was left, that was not set down in his writ; and all the writings were brought to him afterwards.'

The inquiries made by the tax commissioners followed a fairly standard pattern from place to place. The commissioners recorded the name of the village or manor; the name of the tenant in the time of King Edward the Confessor, and the tenant in 1086; the number of *hides* in the manor; the amount of land which could be ploughed; the number of ploughteams actually working on the lord's *demesne* and the number of ploughteams worked by the peasants; the number of *households*; the acreage of meadow and the extent of woodland and pasture; the number of mills, fisheries and various miscellaneous items, together with their annual value; and the total value of the manor both before the Conquest and in 1086.

A *hide* was probably originally an actual amount of arable land, comprising four *virgates* of about thirty acres each; but it had become rather artificial through its use as a unit of rateable value for tax, and by 1086 it no longer necessarily bore much relationship to the real agricultural resources of the village. The *demesne* of the lord of the manor was that part of the estate farmed by him for his own use; the peasants in the village usually had to carry out certain labour services at specified times on the lord's land in addition to farming their own holdings. The peasants were subdivided into several different classes: the *villeins,* who probably held about thirty acres or a virgate each; the *bordars,* who held half that amount; the *cottars,* who held less than a couple of acres; and

The gospel oak in winter.

the *serfs,* whose status was virtually one of slavery.

The Domesday Book was in fact written in two volumes, and Borsetshire is included towards the end of the first folio. The entry for Ambridge reads:

> The Prior of St Mary's, Worcester, holds Ambridge with one berewick. Eadred holds it of him. There are ten hides. There are four ploughlands in demesne with 8 serfs. Eight villeins, 12 bordars, and 2 cottars have 12 ploughs. There is woodland 3 leagues by half a league and five acres of meadow. There is a mill rendering 200 eels annually. In the time of King Edward it was worth 80 shillings, and now 100 shillings.

The Domesday Book record is not always easy to understand, but it does provide the earliest glimpse of the village community and its agricultural background now available to us. The Ambridge entry gives little real evidence of the size of the village – it was a record for tax purposes only. The amount of recorded woodland seems surprisingly large in relation to the known extent of woodland in the parish at a later date and it may be that Ambridge had an interest in woodland resources well outside the present parish – perhaps in the Forest of Am.

8

Ridge and Furrow

Looking down on Ambridge in the evening, as the sun goes down behind the country park and the shadows fall low across the fields, it is suddenly noticeable that a number of pastures are patterned with long stripes, and for an instant the remains of medieval Ambridge spring to view: the open fields with their ridges and furrows created by oxen and the single plough. The remains of ridge and furrow are particularly widespread in Borsetshire and the Midlands, although the renewed ploughing of the 1960s caused the destruction by modern machinery of large areas. Ridge and furrow is not always of any great antiquity, but in many places it can be shown to provide a direct link with the open-field system of the Middle Ages.

The classic view of open-field cultivation is the division of the parish into two or three vast, unhedged fields, subdivided into smaller blocks of land called furlongs, which in turn were divided into strips. Documentary evidence shows that by the later Middle Ages Ambridge had four open fields: West Field, Lakey Hill Field, East Field and Brook Field. (The name of the last survives in the name of Brookfield Farm.) Today there is a fair amount of ridge and furrow left on the former East Field (now Home Farm) and on West Field where the pastures slope up from the Borchester road to the country park. On Lakey Hill and Brookfield, however, the evidence of the past is now slight.

In the Middle Ages, the land worked by the Ambridge peasant was scattered about in single strips all over the parish, so that every peasant got a share of both the good land and the bad. The size of the strips was conditioned by the capacity of the medieval oxteam to pull the plough. The optimum distance, below which too frequent turning wasted effort and beyond which the team became ineffective through tiring, determined the length of the strip and hence of the furlong, and was often about 220 yards. The standard width of the strip was the old rod, pole, or perch of 5½ yards, and its area was thus a rood or quarter-acre. These average measurements would in practice vary greatly – on heavy clay soils, for example, similar to those in most parts of Ambridge, the effectiveness of the ploughteam was reduced and the length of the strip

Ridge and furrow at Grange Farm. This land has been used as a pasture for many years and the medieval field system is clearly visible. Modern methods of deep 'mole' ploughing are slowly eradicating many features of the man-made landscape.

Home Farm with Leader's Wood in the distance. The woodland is the last remnant of the medieval Forest of Am. In Tudor times the three fields seen here were a patchwork of small strips, which were still visible before deep ploughing in the mid-sixties.

correspondingly shorter. The medieval single-mouldboard plough could be used to build up the strip into one or more ridges, and this might be done for a number of reasons: to improve drainage on clay soils, to make a permanently recognizable strip to reduce the chance of disputes, or even simply to increase the surface area under cultivation. Ridge and furrow derived from open field cultivation is often characterized by a pronounced reversed-S curve along its length (West Field and Brookfield both show good examples); this was caused by the plough-team beginning to swing to the left towards the end of each strip in preparation for the turn on the headland.

This feature, together with the height and breadth of the ridges and their lack of relationship to the existing fields – bundles of ridges some-

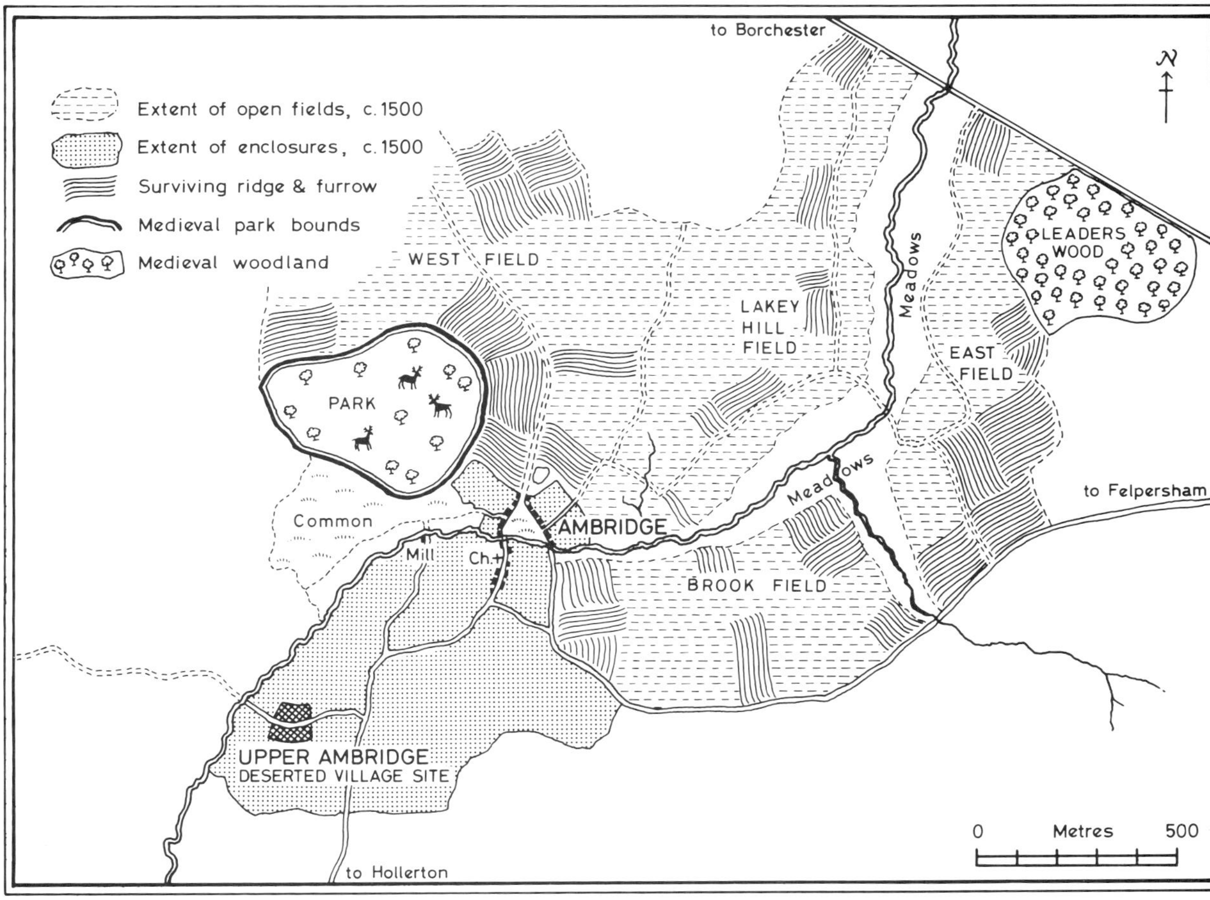

Medieval Ambridge.

times change direction in mid-field and run underneath existing hedges – usually distinguish ridge and furrow from post-enclosure agricultural practices. Narrower, lower, straighter ridges which lie comfortably within the existing fields are, by contrast, likely to be of much more recent date, perhaps a product of nineteenth-century steam ploughing, or a late attempt to improve drainage after enclosure.

In Ambridge many of the fields at Hollowtree and Sawyers Farm have ridges which can be identified as nineteenth-century drainage, although the medieval ridge and furrow must have covered the land originally. Areas which were not under arable cultivation in the Middle Ages can be identified from the lack of ridge and furrow and from documentary sources. Even in a predominantly open field parish like Ambridge, several areas were never cultivated in medieval times. These included the riverside meadows along the Am Valley, the common pasture west of the village, the small medieval park incorporated in the present deer park and the area of ancient woodland at Leader's Wood.

It can be estimated that sixty per cent of ridge and furrow ploughing in Ambridge has been levelled by modern cultivation techniques in the last thirty years.

9

Services due from a Villein on the Manor of Lyttleton

in 1254, from a manuscript now in the possession of Borsetshire County Record Office.

Simon Box holds a messuage and a virgate of land at 7*s* per annum, payable at the four terms, and owes Warselver on St Stephen, and toll for each horse born to him, should it be sold within the manor, 1*d,* and for an ox, and for a pig over a year old 1*d,* and of less age ½*d,* but it may not be a sucking pig. And he cannot sell pork from the Feast of St Peter in chains to that of St Andrew without leave of the lord. He owes help at the ale-making of the lord, that is called fulfthale, and at the ale-making for the lord's cellar, and shall give one silver penny for himself and his wife. He owes toll of ale when he shall brew for sale, 1*d,* and owes help at the Feast of St Michael and hundred selver, and owes heriot at his death, viz, the best animal that he shall have. He owes prison guard in his turn and to lead to Borchestere. He is not able to send away his son, nor to marry his daughter without his lord's leave, and they the jury say that his full rate is 8*s* and that he does no work at any time.

And when he has been at work for all the year then he will be quit of 5*s* and 1*d,* and owes at the Feast of St Andrew 11*d,* and at the Nativity of St John the Baptist 12*d,* and he shall work every week from the Feast of St Michael the Arch to the Feast of St Andrew for one day, viz, to plough and to harrow, to hoe and to reap, or what else he may be ordered at the will of his lord, and in the same manner from the Feast of St Andrew until the Feast of St John. And from the Feast of St John until the Feast of St Michael he shall work every week four days with one man, and at the time of harvest (Messis) every week he shall come with one man to Bederipp (reaping) of the lord until the corn of the lord shall be gathered in. In the meanwhile, if his own corn be harvested before that of his lord, he owes it with one man, or two at his lord's will, to collect his lord's corn assiduously till all shall be collected. And he owes it to cart hay or corn from any virgate as often as the work shall be required.

10

The Deserted Village of Ambridge

The number of villages which survive in England today represent only a proportion of the villages which existed in the Middle Ages, and many parishes contain one (or even two) deserted villages or hamlets. The distribution of such sites is widespread in most parts of England, but they are especially common in some parts of the Midlands.

The reasons for their desertion were many and varied, and are not always easy to determine. Many which disappeared seem to have been the smaller and weaker communities, settled during a period of rising population on poorer, more marginal land which subsequently became untenable during the later medieval economic decline. The Black Death of 1349 destroyed relatively few villages directly, but it had a very considerable indirect effect in opening up the labour market and making it much easier for tenants to abandon holdings in marginal areas and move away to seek a more comfortable living elsewhere. In some cases the role of the landowner was important. Some villages and hamlets – like Ambridge Superior – became deserted in the early Middle Ages through the activities of Cistercian abbeys, who often removed entire settlements to make way for great sheep farms or granges. Later on, in the fifteenth century, many landowners carried out enforced evictions in order to turn over the former arable fields and even the village site itself to permanent pasture for sheep. Later still, particularly in the eighteenth century, the fashion for big houses set in splendid landscaped parks encouraged some of the landlords to remove whole communities from the vicinity of their manor-house and resettle them in 'model' villages outside the walls of the park.

Many sites can still be recognized on the ground. Sometimes the village was big enough to have its own church, which may have outlasted the community it served. Empty parishes with isolated churches in the fields, remote from any existing villages, are widespread in many parts of England. Sometimes the church fell into ruin or was demolished, but not infrequently fragments of window tracery or other sculpture survive, incorporated into later barns or other buildings, as happened at Grange Farm. On many sites slight earthworks reveal the

The deserted village at Grange Farm.

extent and plan of the village, and streets will often survive as a hollow-way; being generally unsurfaced, their level was reduced over a period of time by the passage of traffic. On either side of the street the sites of the houses themselves can often be detected in the form of low platforms, separated by shallow ditches. In some areas stone foundations can be detected, but over much of Borsetshire timber buildings were general throughout the Middle Ages, and only the platform survives. Behind the houses, ditches or banks may surround a whole series of long, rectangular plots, which were the attached crofts and gardens. If there was a manor-house, this can often be recognized as a more complex series of earthwork enclosures, or as a moat. The edge of the village was usually defined by a low boundary bank, beyond which the ridge and furrow of its open fields usually begins.

Such sites are best seen in winter when the grass is at its lowest, and in early morning or late evening when the low sunlight throws the slight mounds and hollows into sharp relief. The recognition and surveying of such sites is urgent, as intensified agricultural practices are resulting in the widespread ploughing-up of the old pasture which had until now survived.

The existence of a second settlement in Ambridge parish was suspected from the Domesday record describing 'Ambridge with one berewick' (a separate hamlet) but it was not until the summer of 1980 that two members of the survey team, riding on Blossom Hill in the evening as the sun was going down, saw the shadows from slight earthworks in the pasture adjacent to Grange Farm.

A check was made with the County Museum Service to see if there were any known aerial photographs of the site (much of Borsetshire is

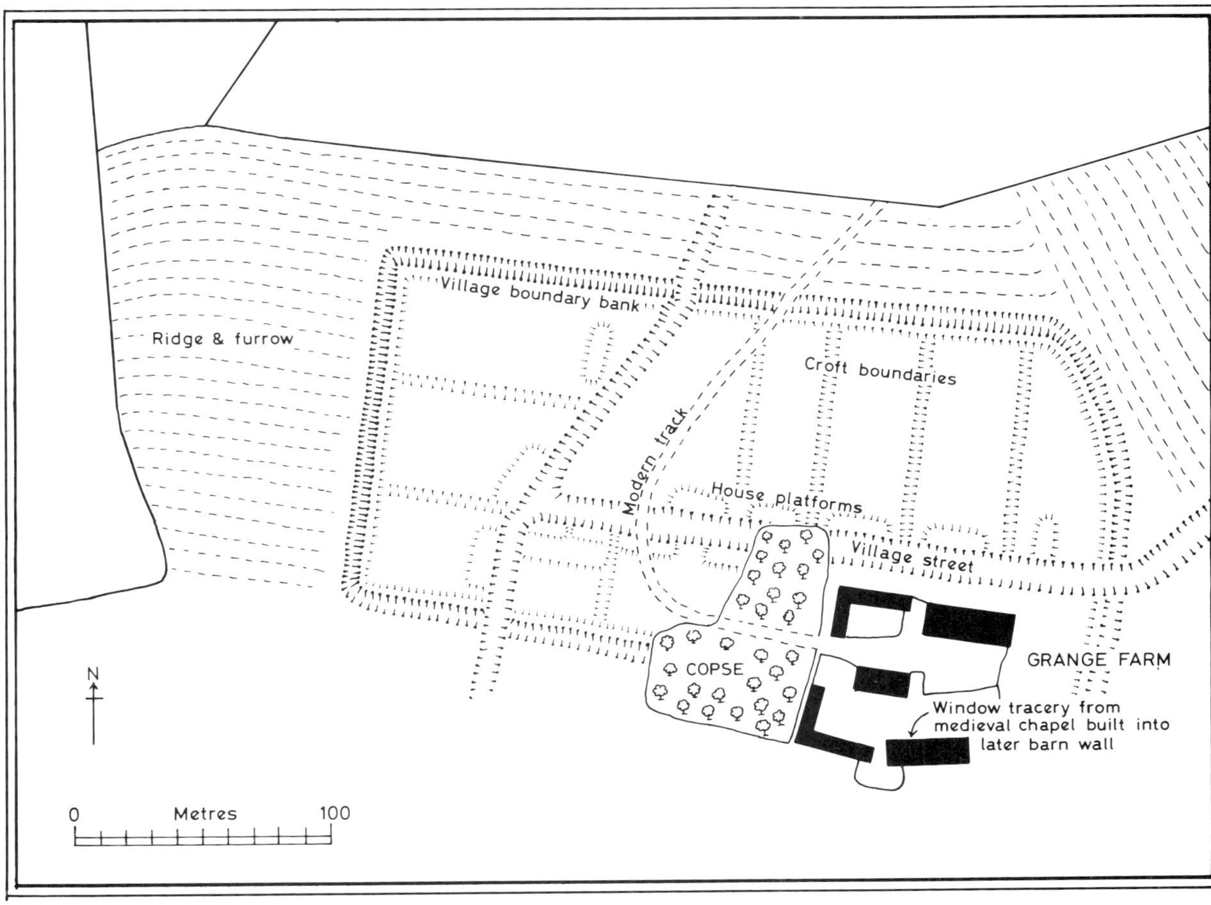

Deserted medieval village site at Grange Farm, Upper Ambridge.

already covered) and when none were found photographs were taken by the survey team from a light aircraft, using specially recommended camera equipment. Results were at first disappointing – the team discovered only by trial and error that for good aerial pictures it is essential to use a plane that can fly slowly with little vibration, which has its wings above the fuselage to avoid interfering with the field of vision, and which can have its fuselage door removed to give the photographer a wide view.

Good photographs were finally produced, which clearly showed Grange Farm pasture to be the site of a former settlement of some kind. The connection between an entry in the Domesday record and a modern photograph of earthworks remained, however, very tenuous. It was strengthened by research at the County Record Office in Felpersham, where the Borsetshire lay subsidy rolls of 1327 and 1332 listed two Ambridges: Ambridge Inferior (or Lower Ambridge) which was by far the larger settlement, and Ambridge Superior (Upper Ambridge).

The archivist at the County Record Office was able to help further by pointing out that the name 'Grange' often indicates the site of a large monastic estate farm. Further documentary research revealed that the Cistercian Abbey of Darrington had acquired the estate of Upper Ambridge south of the river during the thirteenth century. The abbey's account rolls (now in the Public Record Office in London) confirmed that it had a grange at Upper Ambridge on which it was keeping a vast flock of sheep, and this shows that the predominant land use in that part of the parish had changed from arable to pastoral farming before the late fourteenth century. Pastoral farming required a much smaller labour force and the former inhabitants of Upper Ambridge had either dwindled away to seek a living elsewhere or had been forcibly evicted. There are a number of similar cases of village desertions associated with Cistercian sheep farming elsewhere in England.

Many villages and hamlets which are now deserted once had their own churches or chapels, and even if these do not survive in ruined form or converted to other uses, they are often referred to in documentary sources. A brief entry in the Darrington Abbey account roll for 1397–8 records that £3 had been spent on stone for the walls and tiles for the repair of the roof of the chapel of St Margaret in Upper Ambridge, which had fallen into disrepair since the desertion of the hamlet, but was being brought back into use as a chapel for the monastic grange. This would probably have been the only stone building in the original hamlet, the peasant houses being of timber and thatch, and for some time the survey team were hopeful that the chapel might still be found to exist in the cellar and foundations of the present Grange Farm. Some difficulty was found in gaining access to the cellar, but permission to examine it was eventually given by tenant farmer Joe Grundy and the stone walls of the cellar were confirmed to be of eighteenth-century origin, although some of the stone may well have been quarried from the Norman chapel. That the chapel was quarried for other buildings was confirmed in the autumn of 1980, when a pile of scrap iron was cleared away from its position against the wall of one of the barns at Grange Farm, to reveal a blocked stone tracery window of Norman origin.

The earthworks of the site were also surveyed by the group by means of a thirty-metre grid laid out using measuring tapes and ranging poles, and sketching in the mounds and hollows and breaks of slope observed within each square. This revealed a village street showing up as a hollow-way north of the farm buildings, joining another street, roughly at right-angles, to the west. Low platforms were visible alongside both streets, which would have represented the sites of the timber-built peasant houses. Behind the house sites ditches marked the divisions between the separate crofts and the settlement margin was defined by a well marked boundary bank and ditch, beyond which the ridge and furrow of the contemporary field system could be seen. At least ten house sites and crofts could be identified, and several more have probably been obliterated by the present buildings of Grange Farm.

II

Bluebell, Oxlip and English Lime

Areas of woodland in the English landscape may be of very diverse origin. The most recent plantations tend to concentrate on single species, especially conifers, which grow rapidly and fetch a relatively quick return for the investment. Earlier plantations in the eighteenth and nineteenth centuries were often made as much for amenity as commercial reasons, and contain a greater variety of deciduous trees and exotic species newly-introduced into Britain. These occur particularly in the form of ornamental clumps and screes around the parks and grounds of the great houses of the landed aristocracy, to provide a carefully designed landscaped setting for the house itself. Good examples can be seen around the Grey Gables Country Park. Smaller blocks of woodland also appeared in the eighteenth and nineteenth century in the form of shelter-belts and fox coverts. The best local example is Lyttleton Cover.

Some woods, however, have a much earlier origin, maintaining a continuous existence for many centuries, dating back beyond the earliest available records and beyond the life-span of any of the individual trees now surviving. In the Middle Ages such woods were a valuable resource, carefully managed and conserved, to provide oak trunks for building timber and also wattles, fenceposts, hurdles, firewood and a host of other items. Coppicing, the regular cutting of trees down to stump level in order to encourage the roots to produce successive generations of poles, was widely practised. Some woods were also used for grazing of stock; early records often mention 'pannage', the right to allow swine to forage for acorns and mast in the woods. Others were preserved as deer parks by the king or by great landowners in order to supply game for hunting. Where grazing was important, the trees were often managed and exploited by pollarding, whereby they were regularly cut and harvested at a height of a couple of metres above the ground. Much of the woodland in England in the Middle Ages was of post-Roman date, having grown up over previously cultivated land, but some of it may represent an uncleared remnant of the primeval forest which covered all of Britain in the remote prehistoric past.

Medieval wood species in Leader's Wood: bluebell, English limes and wild service tree.

A natural hedgerow, Grange Farm. Oak, elm, blackthorn and hawthorn have seeded themselves along a ditch and fence boundary.

The identification of ancient woodlands is possible in several ways. Large-scale maps may take us back to the sixteenth century, while written records may push the date of some named woods back into the early Middle Ages. Old woodlands, like Leader's Wood, Ambridge, are often located in the far corners and boundaries of the parish and tend to be on poorer soils, where there was less competition from the demands of the plough. In contrast to the rectilinear and geometric shapes of later plantations, they are often irregularly rounded in outline. Their boundaries are often defined by long, sinuous earthworks. If there is a wide ditch within a massive bank, the chances are that the original intention was to provide an enclosure to house deer for hunting; the bank would have been topped by a paling fence, and one or more entrances designed in such a way that deer could enter the enclosure from the surrounding countryside, but could not then get out again. One such medieval deer park forms the nucleus of the present country park. If there is a ditch *outside* the bank, as is the case at Leader's Wood, then the wood itself would have been regarded as the most valuable produce, the function of the boundary being to protect the young coppice shoots from grazing.

Aethelwold's Hedge, which dates from Saxon times, curving round the north-west boundary of Willow Farm.

The botanical content of a wood may also serve as some guide to its antiquity. A wood containing a large variety of native tree species is likely to be much older than one composed of mainly exotics or of only a single species. Some types of tree and shrub are particularly characteristic of ancient woods, such as the wild service tree, the native small-leaved lime and the midland hawthorn, all of which were found in Leader's Wood. The variety of lichens growing on the trees is likely to be much richer in ancient woods than in recent plantations. Certain flowering plants, such as bluebell, wood anemone, dog's mercury, Solomon's Seal, yellow star-of-Bethlehem, herb Paris and oxlip, seem to be restricted to ancient woodlands in some parts of the country, but there is a great deal of regional variation and such indicators must be used with caution: the bluebell, for example, seems to be a fairly reliable guide in the east of England, but in the wetter west it will thrive outside woodlands altogether and will readily colonize recent plantations.

Along with the decline in the traditional management practices of coppicing and pollarding, there has been a massive destruction of ancient woodlands since the Second World War, as they have been

The medieval hedgerow, Five-Acre Field, Brookfield, showing different hedgerow species.

grubbed out for agriculture or replaced by conifer plantations. A wood can be as much of an ancient monument as any ruined abbey or castle, and there is an urgent need for the identification and recording of ancient woods before it is too late.

The intricate mesh of hedges which contributes so much to the attractiveness of the English landscape is also of great interest historically. The use of hedges as field boundaries can be documented back to Anglo-Saxon times, and in Ambridge alone two hedgerows can be said, with some confidence, to belong to this period. It may be that they preserve the line of the boundaries of Romano-British or even prehistoric fields and estates.

In Borsetshire the majority of hedges date from the great transformation of the landscape in the eighteenth and nineteenth centuries, when the processes of parliamentary enclosure broke up the open fields into

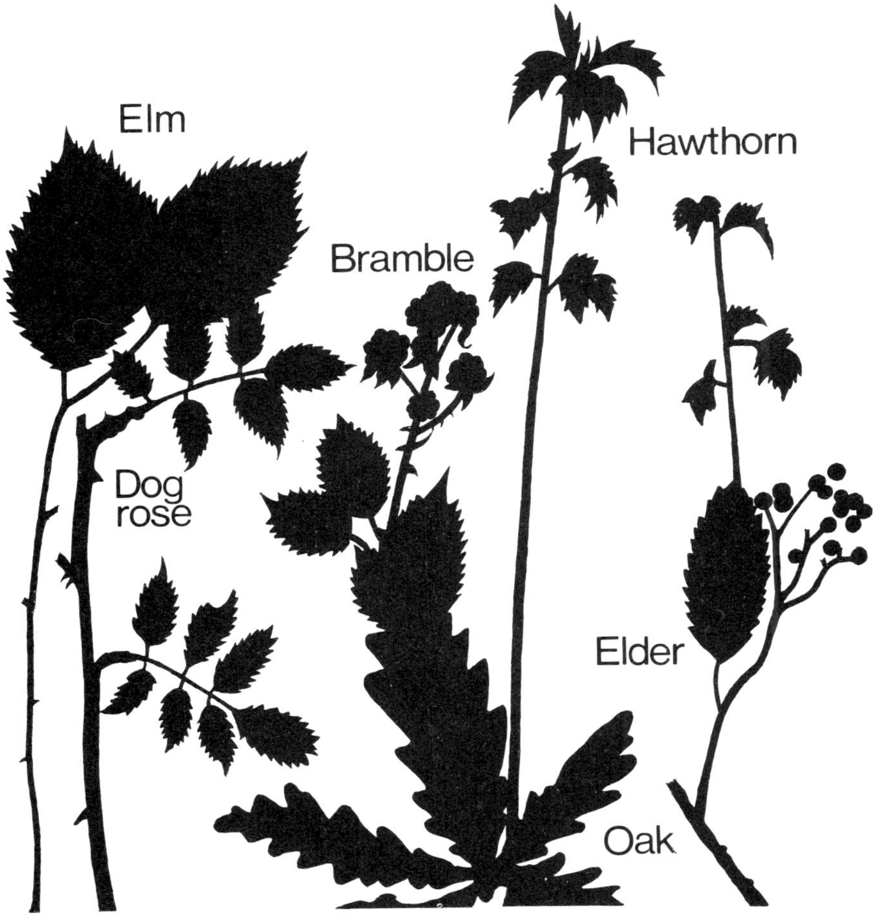

Key

the chequered pattern we know today. The survey was able to show, however, that a minority of hedges in Ambridge, particularly those along parish boundaries, may be very much older.

It is rarely possible to date individual hedges with any precision but certain general indications can be found. Documentary evidence such as charter boundary perambulations (the Ambridge Saxon charter) or maps can show us that a hedge already existed by a particular date, while an enclosure award will give us the earliest date at which hedges in the area described can have made their first appearance in the landscape. Relative dates can sometimes be established by examining the relationship between different hedges – a hedge following a long, continuous, direct or gently sinuous course over some distance is likely to be earlier than other hedges joining it at right-angles but not crossing it. Field shapes are an important clue. Small, very irregularly-shaped fields may be the product of piecemeal woodland clearance in the Middle Ages, and the hedges may be simply uncleared strips of wood. Long fields with their sides curved in the form of a reversed-S will usually be the result of enclosure by agreement amongst freeholders around the seventeenth century, when the general outlines of the open-field strips were 'fossilized' in the new hedged boundaries. Grid-iron patterns of square or rectangular fields of uniform size will usually date from parliamentary enclosures of the eighteenth and nineteenth centuries.

In recent years it has been realized that the botanical content of a hedge may also help to date it. Working from the basic principle that the longer a hedge has been in existence, the greater the number of shrub species likely to be growing in it, a convenient rule of thumb has been developed. By counting the number of different shrub species in a thirty-metre length of hedge and then taking an average of several samples from the same hedge, it has been suggested that each additional species represents another century of the hedge's existence: thus, a single-species hedge containing only, say, common hawthorn, is unlikely to be much more than a hundred years old, while one with five different species might date back to the Tudor period. In many areas certain species, such as the midland hawthorn, field maple and spindle, are restricted to the older hedges. This dating method is very imprecise, as all sorts of factors can intervene to upset the 'one species per hundred years' formula; nonetheless it often helps in the distinguishing of an Anglo-Saxon hedge from a Tudor one, or a Tudor hedge from a nineteenth-century one.

The investigation of hedgerows is an urgent task, for the demands of modern agricultural machinery mean that it is now uneconomic to work smaller fields, and so hundreds of miles of hedge have been grubbed out in recent years. Not only is this a loss to the scenery and detrimental to wild life, it is also a major loss of historical evidence.

In Ambridge, the survey team found that the hedges along the parish boundary appear to be the oldest. Those which can be identified with Eadric's Ditch and Aethelwold's Hedge of the 936 charter, and the roadside hedge south of the old Five Acre Field on Brookfield Farm on the southern boundary of the parish each contain between ten and twelve shrub species. The vicinity of Grange Farm in the south-west of the parish, which was enclosed in the early fourteenth century, has a number of hedges with five or six shrub species. Elsewhere in the parish the hedges are predominantly of common hawthorn or blackthorn and surround spare and rectangular fields typical of the parliamentary enclosures of the eighteenth and nineteenth centuries.

12

Medieval Taxes

The lay subsidy rolls of 1327 and 1332 are among the few documentary sources we have to help us picture Medieval Ambridge – and like the Domesday survey, the rolls are a very dangerous guide. They are tax returns only and give no indication of the number of people who managed to avoid paying tax or who were too poor to pay.

In theory, anyone with movable goods to the value of ten shillings or more was liable to taxation. The tax rate in 1327 was one shilling in the pound. The money was levied largely so that Queen Isabella, 'the she-wolf of France', and her lover Mortimer (they had caused Edward II to be murdered in Berkeley Castle) could pay a war indemnity to France and the lay subsidy roll shows twenty-three people in Ambridge Inferior and ten people in Ambridge Superior liable to tax. The total paid by the people of Ambridge Inferior – the main village as we know it now – was £3 0s 10d, an average of 2s 7d per person taxed; and Ambridge Superior paid 7s 8d, an average of 9d per person. This suggests that the inhabitants of the Grange Farm settlement were noticeably poorer than villagers in the main settlement.

In 1332, the young Edward III had seized power from his mother Queen Isabella and hanged her lover Mortimer, and was determined to avenge the battle of Bannockburn by taking an army into Scotland. Ambridge (Inferior and Superior) was required to pay tax yet again – this time at the rate of 1s 4d in the pound. While twenty-five people in Ambridge Inferior paid (two more than in 1327), only six paid in Ambridge Superior, indicating that the inhabitants of the Grange Farm settlement were either on the tax border-line or capable of practising a substantial and successful degree of tax evasion.

By 1344 the tax roll indicates a change in the system of collection. Villages were required to find a certain sum of money, and details of the levy were left to the local tax collector. The revenue demanded for Ambridge (Superior and Inferior) was £4 11s 0d, indicating either the greed of government or the increasing prosperity of the two villages.

The tax revenue fixed in 1344 remained the same for a hundred and eighty years, a monument not to the spending policies of the exchequer

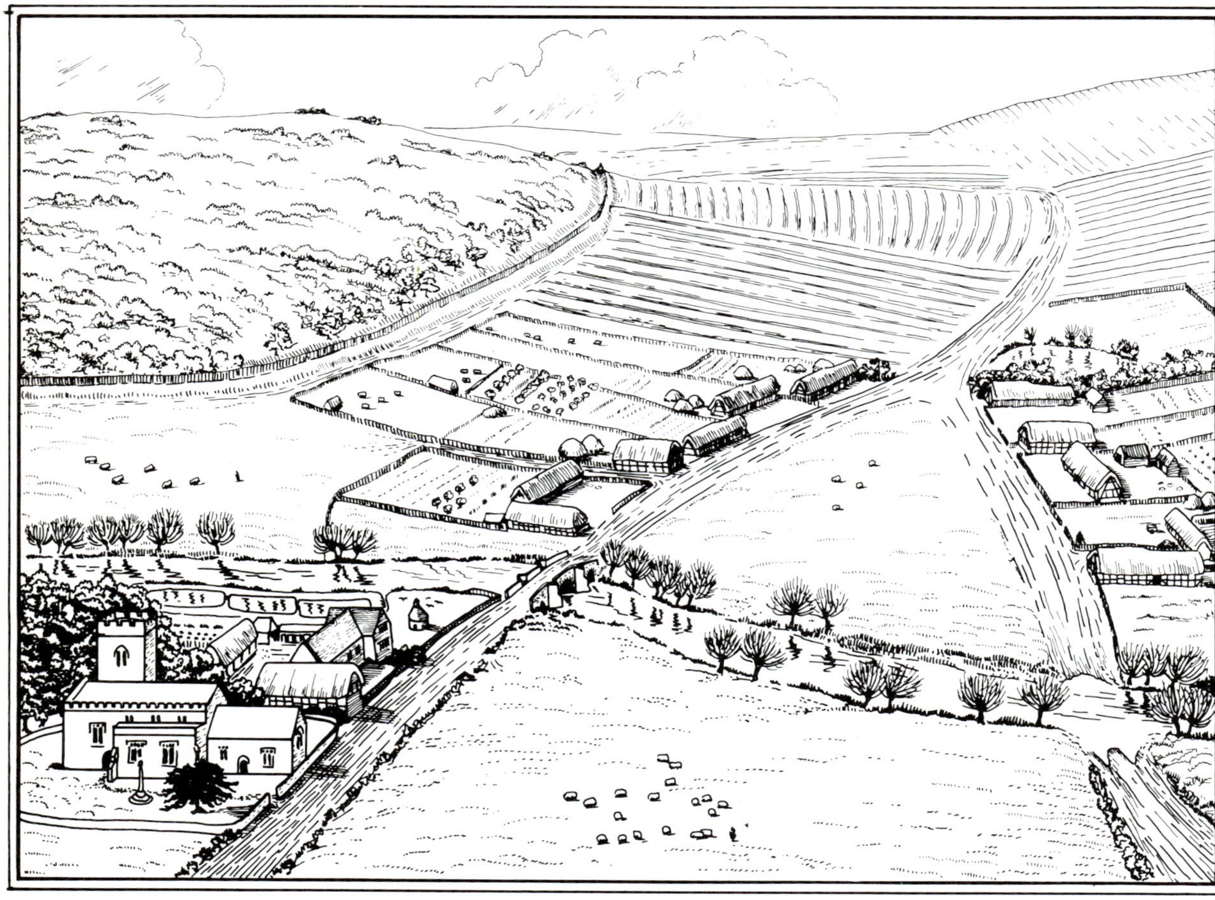

Reconstruction of Ambridge in the later Middle Ages.

but to the terrible ravages of the Black Death. A third of the population of Europe died and a tax return of 1433 indicates that Ambridge suffered as severely as any other village. Eighty-five years after the plague had entered England, the village appealed against the levy of £4 11s 0d on the grounds that there were insufficient inhabitants to pay such a sum. A reduction of 10s 9d was granted.

13

The Parish Church of St Stephen

In *Antiquities of Borsetshire* Osborne refers to Ambridge church in only one sentence: 'The church was dedicated to St Stephen in Anno 1291 in the reign of Edward First, and was valued at XXVIII Marks; but in the reign of Henry Eighth at no more than XIII *li* vi *s* viii *d*.' Elsewhere, however, Osborne tells us that St Augustine built six churches in the area, of which Ambridge and Loxley Barratt were two.

The present church at Ambridge was built on the site of the early seventh-century St Augustine church and was consecrated in 1281, ten years before its dedication. Architecturally it is a combination of Saxon, late Norman and early English and Perpendicular styles.

The chancel has a fine example of a priest's doorway (eleventh-century) in the south wall. The north wall is early thirteenth-century, the south is fifteenth-century and the east is a mixture of both. Also in the chancel are two fifteenth-century benches.

The altar of stone was added to the church in 1842 and the heads were carved to match those on the font.

The font is octagonal and is contemporary with the rest of the church. It is of carved stone, very ornate and enriched with carved human heads and flowers. It is believed to have been a gift to the church by Edward I and two of the heads are thought to be those of the King and Queen Eleanor of Castille.

The nave has an early thirteenth-century north arcade. The windows, one in the west wall and one west of the porch in the south wall, are both late fourteenth-century, although the west wall of the nave and the south portion of the tower wall forming part of the nave are late thirteenth-century..

The Lawson Chapel, or south transept, was added in the early sixteenth century. The Lawson family bought the manors of Ambridge and Lyttleton in 1472 and during the reign of Henry VII Richard Lawson depopulated Lyttleton and enclosed the Manor Farm lands to the east of the parish. The south transept was probably built by him and the alabaster tomb of himself and his wife Ann occupies most of the chapel. Round the tomb are figures depicting his seven daughters, all of whom

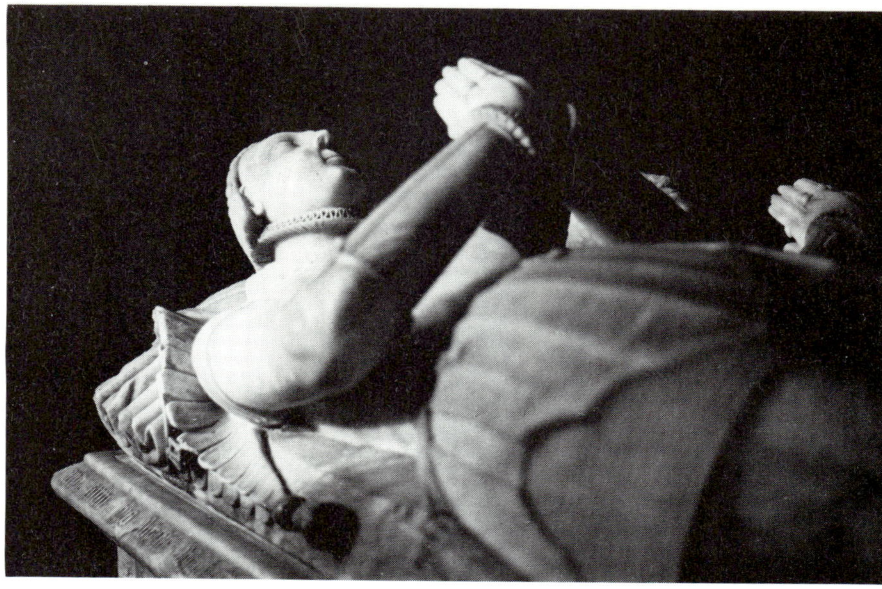

The alabaster tomb of Richard Lawson and his wife Ann in the south transept.

made excellent marriages. Also in the south transept is an ancient communion table of the early seventeenth century.

The tower is fifty-six feet high and leans over six inches to the west. It has no regular foundations, even though the walls are ten feet thick. When rebuilt in the reign of Elizabeth the First, the first and second floor rooms were built as priest's chambers. The first floor room has a fireplace and a fifteenth-century door. The bells were rehung in 1975.

Until 1934 there were three chained books in the church, but these are now held in safe custody by Borsetshire County Record Office. They are *Treatise of Erasmus,* 1548, *Common Places of Christian Religion,* 1578, and *Sermon of John Jewel,* 1611. The Record Office also holds the church registers from 1599 to 1837. The valuable church silver is lodged in the bank and includes an Elizabethan chalice with cover.

During the medieval period the benefice of Ambridge was in the possession of the Abbey of Darrington, which received the greater tythes of corn, hay and wool, and appointed a vicar to serve the parish. The vicar had thirty acres of glebe land set aside for his support, together with lesser tythes, mortuary fees and oblations at the principal feasts. In 1291 Pope Nicholas IV ordered a tax survey of the parishes of England and Ambridge was said to be worth £5 6s 8d a year. The vicar received tythe income to the value of £3 6s 8d a year.

Stuart tythes are known in some detail because of the survival of a 'terrier' – a sort of inventory – compiled in 1616. The vicar at this time had thirty-six acres of arable and pasture land and five acres of meadow, and there also belonged to the vicarage 'five pairs of houselings and one barne containg fore bayes'. The vicarage itself is recorded in detail in the probate inventory of John Weston, vicar, who died in 1597. His

St Stephen's Church, Ambridge.

house had a hall, parlour, study, three bedchambers, a kitchen, dairy, two butteries, a brewing house and tythe barn.

The 1616 terrier shows that the vicar was entitled to the lesser tythes, described as being, 'Calves, lambes woole, pigges, egges and fruit . . . and of hemp and flaxe if the ground be digged whyreon it is sowed, also of woode sold.' There was also the Easter oblation of 5d per household – 2d for 'every man an householder, 2d his wife, and 1d for the garden in lieu of herbage, rootes and flowers, as it is and hath ben usialle by ancient custom.'

The tythe of calves and lambs depended on how many animals had been born to each particular farmer. The man with seven calves gave the fourth to the vicar, and received 1½d in payment. If he had eight calves he received only a penny, only a half penny if nine calves and no compensation at all if he had ten or more. Local farmers clearly discovered a way to avoid the tythe by grazing other people's animals on their land, because the terrier has an additional and rather extraordinary clause rebuking attempts at tythe evasion and laying down a scale of one farthing per animal pastured in winter and then sold elsewhere, and charges for spring and summer grazing.

Churchwardens accounts also survive for the year 1618 (they are kept, with the 1616 terrier, at Borsetshire Record Office). They show that the parish made most of its income from renting out church property, including the upstairs floor of the 'church-house', the renting out of pews, the charge for burials (6s 8d) and fines for swearing, drunkenness and, in this year at least, a fine for the 'keeping of an unlicenced alehouse'. The enormous sum of £8 4s 11d was raised from the Ambridge and Lyttleton 'church ales' – a kind of parish feast that lasted all day. The churchwardens arranged for maltsters to supply free malt, and beer was brewed and bread baked in the church-house. Parishioners contributed eggs, butter, cheese and fruit. During the day of church ales the regular alehouse was ordered to be closed and the villagers were exhorted by the vicar to eat and drink zealously in aid of parish funds.

In March and October 1618 the churchwardens paid 6d to have the church strewn with rushes and also in October they paid 1s for winter coals for the church and received a gift of charcoal and incense to sweeten the air. 23 July has the item '6d per week for Agnes and bastard': by the poor law of 1601 the overseers of the poor and the churchwardens were required, in the case of bastardy, to discover the father of the child and order him to pay 8d a week for the upkeep of mother and child. If the suspected father was not to be traced, the burden could be placed on relations or even grandparents. When all else failed – as in the case of Agnes and her child – support had to be granted out of parish funds.

Several of the gravestone inscriptions in Ambridge church and churchyard show the work of rural poets through the centuries.

All you that do this day pafs by,
As you are now, fo once was I,
As I am now fo fhalt you be,
Therefore prepare to follow me.

E. Blower, 1710

Here lie Paul and Richard Fenn,
Two lawyers, yet two honest men.
God works miracles now and again.

21 June, 1746

My anvil and hammer lies declined,
My bellows have quite lost their wind,
My fire's extinct, my forge decay'd,
My vice is in the dust all laid.
My coals is spent, my iron gone,
My nails are drove, my work is done,
My mortal part rests night this stone,
My soul to heaven, I hope is gone.

Thomas Salter, Blacksmith of
Ambridge, d 12 June, 1784

Here lyeth the Body of Walter Bloom, of Ambridge
a dyer, who departed this life the first day of
October Anno Dom 1705.
Tho wee have loft our faithful friend,
In Christ wee hope he made his end,
His Body in the Grave doth rest,
To rife wee hope forever bleft.

The information that Walter Bloom was a dyer is intriguing, giving a hint that there may have been some rural industry in Ambridge in the early eighteenth century. It is more likely, however, that Bloom worked in Borchester or Felpersham, where cloth-making was well established, and returned home to Ambridge in his old age.

The dues owing to the clerk to the Parochial Church of Ambridge in 1735 are also detailed in a terrier now kept in the Records Office:

Every plowgate	4*d*
Every householder	2*d*
For every burial and tolling the Bell	1*s* 8*d*
For every woman churched	4*d*
For every corps brought out of another parish to be buried and tolling the bell	3*s* 4*d*
For the same for a corps taken out of this parish to be buried in another	3*s* 4*d*
The same has been given for a corps in church	
For every marriage by banns	1*s* 0*d*
For every marriage by licence	2*s* 6*d*

14

Village Families

There are four family names that recur time after time in the parish history of Ambridge: the Blowers, the Archers, the Forrests and the Gabriels. In the Victorian age, when the Sick and Provident Society held its annual club day, a village forefather or 'lord' was elected to head the festivities, and was always chosen from one of the above families.

An Ambridge churchyard survey was made by members of the Women's Institute in 1980 as part of a national survey being organized by the WI, and the result showed the name Blower occurring eleven times (the first in 1710), Archer seven times (the first 1832), Forrest seven times (1834) and Gabriel five times (1839). The eighteenth-century inscriptions – there are four for the Blower family – are all on graves to the left of the main path to the church door, and the absence of any inscriptions previous to 1830 in the main part of the churchyard makes it clear that the ground was levelled around this time and reusage began. The parish register and list of churchwardens establish that all four families were strongly represented in the village from 1750 onwards.

Previous to the mid-eighteenth century, it is difficult to trace any family through documentary evidence. The names of small tenant farmers and artisans rarely had cause to be set down on paper or parchment. The Lawson family rent roll is now kept in the Hope Collection at Bristol, but is incomplete. Often the name of the farm is used rather than the tenant, and many records were destroyed by John Lawson in 1697. An account book covering the period 1640 to 1647 does show, however, that a J. Blower was tenant of Bull Farm.

The Lawson family itself can be traced back to 1472 when Simon Lawson bought the manors of Ambridge and Lyttleton. The name Hope was added in 1699 when Bristol merchant Joseph Hope insisted on the adoption of his name before he would agree to leave the bulk of his fortune to his grandson Charles, the only child of Annabel Hope, his daughter, and John Lawson who died in 1697. John Lawson left the Lawson Estate on the verge of bankruptcy.

The Lawson-Hope family continued as Lords of the Manor until the

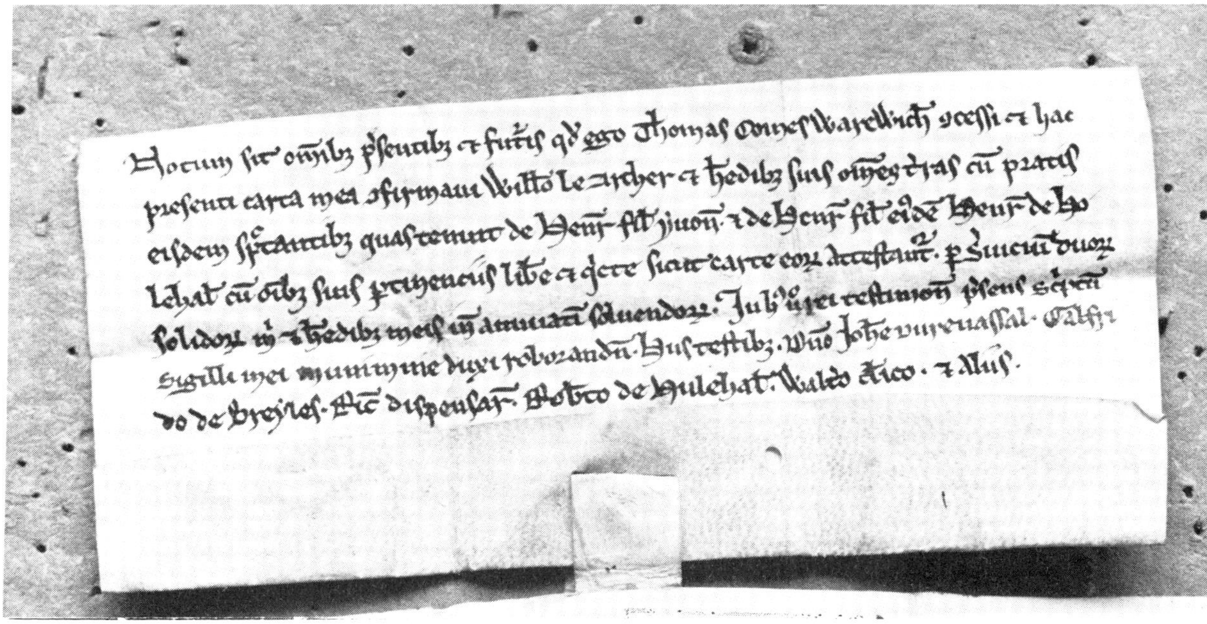

Confirmation from Thomas Earl of Warwick to William le Archer of all the lands and meadows which the said William held of Henry son of Ivo and Henry son of the same Henry de Hulehal; to hold the same rendering annually to the earl two shillings. Witnesses: Sir John Durevassal, Geoffrey de Breyles, Richard Dispensario, Robert de Hulehal, Walter the clerk, and others.

estate was sold in 1954. Lettie Lawson-Hope, the last of the family line, died in 1958.

Attempts to trace the four 'village' families back beyond the eighteenth century met with mixed success. A Richard Blower of Hollerton is mentioned in the will of Thomas Marney in 1557 and one William Forrest is a witness to an inventory of 1586. A Gabriel and a Blower are recorded as having left the village to fight in the King's army in 1642.

Going back to the first development of hereditary surnames in England (they were scarcely known before the Norman Conquest) a Guy de Ferester (1203) and Reginald filius Gabrieli (1212) are named in Curia Regis rolls and the name Robert le Archere is named on a pipe roll of 1166. All three are connected to Borsetshire and although the names are French, there is no real reason to suppose they were not Anglo-Saxon: it had become a widespread practice for Saxon parents to give their children French names. The first connection with Ambridge, however, cannot be made until 1235 when William le Archer was granted the tenancy of an unspecified land-holding by Thomas Earl of Warwick. A Lyttleton Manor court roll of Henry VII's reign mentions a John Archer who paid 4d rent on his mill.

The name William Gabriele is included in the lay subsidy roll of 1332, but the other principal names in the village at the time were Sharpe, Martyn, Gille and Bence. The Archer family must either have lost their land holding during the preceding century or practised a successful degree of tax evasion.

The Forrest family appears consistently in parish records from the early seventeenth century onwards. In the early eighteenth century at

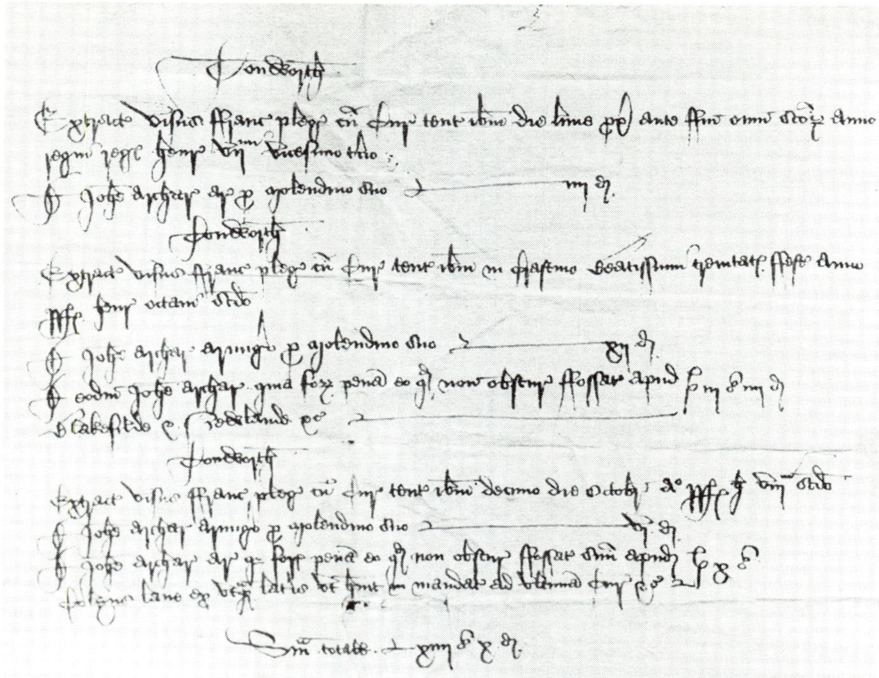

Extract from the view of frankpledge and manor court held on the Monday next before the feast of All Saints in the twenty-third year of the reign of Henry VII. John Archer paid for his mill 4d.

least one member of the family fell on hard times, according to a justice's order made out in Borchester in 1725:

> To the Constable and Churchwarden, the Overseers of the Poor of the parish of Ambridge, greeting. Whereas complaint hath been made unto me, Matthew Pargitter, one of His Majesty's Justices of the Peace, that Geo Forrest of your village, who appears to me to be an inhabitant legally settled in your said parish, is in great need and poverty and likely to perish for want of employment to maintain his wife and family . . .
>
> These are therefore in His Majesty's name to command you to set ye said Geo Forrest to work or pay unto him 2*s* weekly forth out of your publick levey for ye use of ye Poor, otherwise to come before me and show cause to the contrary. Hereof fail not at your peril.

The order was made out a year before the establishment of the Ambridge Poor House, a small cottage set aside for the elderly who were incapable of looking after themselves, the unemployed and homeless and several orphaned children. The account for 1732 shows that money was expended by the Overseer of the Poor to provide 'taters', 'turnopes' and occasionally a cheese. At Christmas there was an extra item of a sheep's head. The following year a glimmer of humanity appears in the item: 'Paid for 12 pound of cherries for ye children of ye house . . . 6*d*.'

Judging by the evidence of names alone, it would seem that the Archer family can claim to be the oldest in the village, going back as it does to the land grant of 1235. Archer, however, is a common name and there is a tradition, recounted to Dan Archer by his mother, that the first Daniel Archer arrived in the village as a penniless wanderer, accompanied by his wife and a child-in-arms, and had to be supported out of poor relief by the parish overseer. (This is itself unlikely as parishes were required only to support their own inhabitants.) Daniel Archer, it was said, was given a job as a day-worker at Hollowtree Mill and the family lived in great poverty until money arrived from relations in Warwickshire which enabled them to buy the tenancy of a smallholding.

From the will of Andrew Archer of Umberslade Hall in the parish of Tamworth in the county of Warwick. 'And whereas my son Daniel Archer by reason of his mean capacity I do believe him not capable to . . . make any provision for any Wife or Children that he may have I do therefore hereby revoke and make void all the Grants and Legacies which I have given my said son Daniel Archer by any of my former wills . . .'.

The poor relief accounts from 1737 to 1782 no longer exist but in 1981 Shula Archer made an attempt to trace a connection with Warwickshire and discovered the will of Andrew Archer of Umberslade Hall, Tamworth, which refers to a Daniel Archer as having been cut off without a penny.

If the present Archer family only came to Ambridge in the 1760s it would seem that the original family died out some time during the preceding two hundred years. The evidence is too flimsy to draw any firm conclusions, but it may well be that the Gabriels are the longest surviving family in the village. Gabriel is not a particularly common name and its incidence in the 1332 lay subsidy roll makes it a strong possibility that the present Walter Gabriel is descended from the William Gabriele of the fourteenth century. If the village club day were to be revived with its customary festivities, Walter Gabriel or his son Nelson could reasonably lay claim to the traditional title of 'lord' of Ambridge.

15

From the Will of Thomas Marney, a prosperous Ambridge yeoman, 1557

(Marney's Farm, between Willow Farm and Hollowtree Farm on the southern slopes of Lakey Hill, is now part of Ambridge Farmers Ltd)

In Dei nomine Amen. The xxiii day of July in the yere of our Lord God a thousand five hundred fifty sevenne, I Thomas Marney of Ambridge, seke in body hole of mynde and remembraunce, make my testament in this maner of wise hereafter folowing. First I bequethe my soule to Almightye God to our Lady Saint Mary and to all the Company of hevynne, and my body to be buried in the Churche Yarde of St Stephen. Also I bequethe to the high awter of St Stephen vii*d*, and to the sacrament of the said awter to have a clothe of silke xx*d*. Item I bequethe to have a prest to serve in St Stephen Church for my fader and moder and me with all my goode frendes oon yere viii markes. Item I bequethe to Agnes my wife vi oxen, x kyne, xii yong beastes, vi horses and mares, my best cart with the harneyse, and alle the householde stuff that she had before I maried her, and the encrease of my duffe house in Penny this oon yere, and all my olde malt except two quarters. Item I bequethe to my brother John Marney fyve score shepe, oon heiffer, two quarters of whete and two quarters of malt and the money that Richard Blower of Hollerton oweth me whiche is x*s*. Item I bequethe to Agnes my doughtere a fetherbed, iix paire of shetes and a shete with a blake seme, a pair of beads that were my moders, xi pewter disshes, fyve hundred shepe and xl beasts. To Dorathe my doughtere a fetherbed, iix pair of shetes, ffyve hundred shepe and xl beasts. And the said Agnes and Dorathe to have between them vi silver spones.

16

Borsetshire dialect

Shakespeare in Borsetshire

Titania: Or say, sweet love, what thou desirest to eat?
Bottom: Truly, a peck of provender; I could munch your good dry oats. Methinks I have a great desire to a bottle of hay.

The request of Bottom for a 'bottle' of hay (*A Midsummer Night's Dream,* IV, i) is an example of Shakespeare's obvious familiarity with the Borsetshire dialect. Clearly he travelled at least one road out of Stratford other than the road to London, although there are no records or traditions which connect him with the county. The Borsetshire dialect was first collected together by the Reverend A.S. Pargetter in the eighteen fifties, but a number of dialect words used by Shakespeare – including 'bottle' for a measure of hay – were included in J.R. Wise's *Shakespeare: His Birthplace and Its Neighbourhood,* published in 1861.

Wise was primarily concerned with the Warwickshire dialect, but about thirty Borsetshire words were allowed to creep in – several others being known to both counties. He only listed those words which were commonly used in the Midland shires at the time he was writing, and it is rather distressing to realize that almost all of them have died out during the past hundred and twenty years. Wise, for example, found the old Borsetshire word 'bavin' (meaning an accumulation of wood chips) to be in everyday use, as indeed it was in Elizabethan England: 'Rash bavin wits, new kindled, and soon burnt' (*1 Henry IV,* III, ii). But the word is now unknown, at least in the area of Ambridge and Penny Hassett, and none of the eighteen eldest inhabitants of the two villages could remember having heard it. Numerous other words which were used by Shakespeare and still enjoyed common usage in the second half of the nineteenth century are now forgotten. They include: 'biggen' – a child's cap; 'Whose brow with homely biggen bound' (*2 Henry IV,* IV, iv): 'rid' – to destroy; 'The Red plague rid you' (*The Tempest,* I, ii): 'noul' – head; 'Ass's noul' (*A Midsummer Night's Dream,* II, ii): 'batlet' – a beater used in washing, sometimes called a dolly or maiden (*As You Like It,* II, iv): 'customer' – a common woman (*Othello,*

Manor Court, drawn in 1820.

IV, iv): 'dup' – to fasten or 'sneck' the door (*Hamlet,* IV, v): 'salt' – a loose woman, as applied to Cleopatra (*Antony and Cleopatra,* II, i): 'squash' – an unripe pea-pod (*A Winter's Tale,* I, ii and *A Midsummer Night's Dream,* III, i): 'loggatts' – an old Borsetshire game similar to skittles (*Hamlet,* V, i).

Research during 1979 and early 1980 showed that in Ambridge itself only a handful of the Borsetshire dialect words used by Shakespeare and recorded by Wise are still known – and only one, 'keck', is in common use, to describe a variety of umbelliferous field weed. Other words are dimly remembered. Dan Archer can recall his wife comparing a woollen hat favoured by her sister-in-law to 'a statute cap' – a curious survival, harking back to 1571 when woollen caps were ordered to be worn by statute in order to encourage the woollen trade, and mentioned by Shakespeare in *Love's Labour's Lost,* V, ii.

Other words recognized, if not in common usage, include: 'whip-stock' for a carter's whip handle, 'Malvolio's nose is no whip-stock' (*Twelfth Night,* II, iii) and 'urchin' for a hedgehog (*Titus Andronicus,* II, iii) – this word is still used by Ambridge's oldest inhabitant, Walter Gabriel, who is also familiar with 'childing' meaning pregnant (*Midsummer Night's Dream,* II, ii). Dan Archer, who is only six weeks younger than Walter Gabriel – they were both born in 1896 – can remember the word 'eanlings' being applied to lambs that had just 'eaned' or dropped (*Merchant of Venice,* I, iii) and 'brize' being the name given to gad-flies (*Antony and Cleopatra,* III, viii). Several villagers can remember how Silas Winter used the phrase 'fore-wearied' when he was tired (*King John,* II, i) and called a bundle of sticks for the fire a 'fardel' (*A Winter's Tale,* IV, iii). Dan Archer was also able to recollect that a former farm worker at Brookfield farm, Simon Cooper, used the phrase 'pick-thanking work' for someone who carried tales (*1 Henry IV,* III, ii) and used the word 'claw', meaning to flatter, 'Look how he claws him' (*Love's Labour's Lost,* IV, ii).

Common Borsetshire dialect words

Over a century ago, when the Reverend A.S. Pargetter compiled his *Borsetshire Words and Phrases,* he referred to the 'fast-fading customs, and superstitions, and proverbs, and phrases, which have been interwoven in our national life, and without which no real history of our strangely mixed people can ever be completely written.' That was in 1854*, and even then, before the spread of a common literacy or even the railway (which did not reach Hollerton until 1856), and almost a century before the invention of the wireless, the Reverend Pargetter was alarmed by the way old customs and words were dying out. It is hard, looking back, to understand why, in the eighteen fifties, local customs and traditions should have been weakened. In Ambridge, Emily Winter, who died in 1949, used to recount how she heard her grandmother saying that as a child she was fourteen before she paid her first visit to Borchester, and only went as far afield as Felpersham once in her life.

Perhaps the Borsetshire dialect has been in decline ever since the days of Saxon England. What was certain about the eighteen fifties, however, was the new interest in dialect and folk-lore among the educated classes. The work of the English Dialect Society, the patient research of Miss Jackson and Miss Burne in their *Shropshire Folk-Lore* and the glossary of Warwickshire dialect compiled by Thomas Sharp of Coventry enable us to compare Pargetter's Borsetshire dialect with the usage in surrounding counties.

True dialect has now almost vanished. The casual visitor to the Griffin's Head in Penny Hassett or the Bull in Ambridge is unlikely to hear the locals saying: 'I'll shog that welly-swatched shackling yawnups!' as he might well have done a century ago, and if he did hear he certainly would not understand what was being said. (I'll shake that dirty, idle, ignorant fellow.) Below are a few of the words that have failed to survive until the present day, and an even smaller list of words which are still alive in the Borchester area.

Pronunciation: The diphthong 'ea' is generally pronounced as a long 'a' in Ambridge – 'plase' for please, 'mate' for meat, 'wake' for weak. The vowel 'o' is sounded as 'u' – 'sung' for song, 'wunst' for once. In many cases the final consonant is also dropped, and 'fun' for found and

*Pargetter's small volume was extended into the more commonly known *Borsetshire Dialect* by his son Edmund Pargetter for the English Dialect Society in 1869.

'pun' for pound are commonly heard among the older village inhabitants. The letter 'd' is softened into 'j', as 'juke' for duke and 'jed' for dead. The nominative and accusative cases are perpetually confounded: 'They ought to have spoken to we'; 'Her told him so'; 'Us won't hurt her, will us?'

Borsetshire dialect words still in common use in 1854:

blench – a glimpse
colly – black
deaf nut – a nut with no kernel
doddered – a pollarded tree
dumble – a small wood in a hollow
footing – foot-ale on working at a new place
glir – to glide on ice
goslings – bloom of willow
gloom – fat or greasy
hocketimon – cut out sides of hay rick
Jack banniel – a tadpole
joistings – the keep of an animal out at grass
moikin or moukin – a scarecrow
moil – to work hard
padded – dry on top, applied to land
pikel – pitchfork
raggle – to succeed
sad – heavy, used when speaking of bread
shackling – idle, loitering
shog – shake or throw off
slinge – lazy
sprunt – a struggle
swagger – to satisfy
token – a death sign
welly-swatched – dirty
unked – melancholy
whamp – to beat a child
yawnups – an ignorant fellow

Borsetshire dialect words still known in the Ambridge area in 1980:

arsy-versy – topsy turvy
badger – a seller
breed and seed – a person's birth and parentage, generally used disparagingly: 'What can you expect, with his bread and seed? Bad 'uns and always have been.'
faggot – a female
haunty – of a horse full of spirit
lace – to beat
mummock – to pull about or worry
plash – to cut and bend down a hedge
pither – to snatch, pet, or fondle

reckling – the last born
slommock – an untidy person
swarm – to climb a tree
sword – the skin of a side of bacon
up and told – to relate a narrative
urchin – a hedgehog

Some common names for birds are:
proud Taylor – goldfinch
dipchick – water-hen
black-a-top – black-cap
Jack Squealer – swift
hickle – woodpecker
hewsick – flycatcher
piefinch (or pinkfinch) – chaffinch
grecian – yellowhammer

(Several of these names of birds were remembered by Tom Forrest, who has worked as a gamekeeper in Ambridge all his life. The common word for the yellowhammer is perhaps the most curious. Mr Forrest believes it originates from the Greek letters which are supposed to appear on the yellowhammer's eggs.)

17

Inventories of the goods of George Boddy, husbandman of Hollowtree, and John Robyns, carpenter, of Ambridge

Probate inventories were required by ecclesiastical courts from the sixteenth to the eighteenth century, the object being to protect executors from excessive claims and next of kin from fraud. Two Tudor inventories relating to Ambridge survive in the records of the Borchester Consistory and Archdeaconry Courts – those of George Boddy and John Robyns. The inventories were usually drawn up by neighbours immediately after the funeral.

1. George Boddy, husbandman of Hollowtree, taken 6 April, 1584 by John Humfrey and William Bagg.

In the haule	
One table a cubberde 2 bordes 2 stooles and a chayre	13.4*d*
In the chamber	
2 bedstedes 2 coffers 2 bedclothes a pyllowe and one boulster	7.0*d*
3 payre of sheetes one Table clothe one tablenapkyne 2 towels and 2 payre pyllowbers	12.0*d*
Thre barrels 2 buckets and other trashe	4.0*d*
2 braspottes one ketle and a candlesticke	6.8*d*
6 platters one sauser and 2 saultes	5.0*d*
Hys Apparrell	6.8*d*
Thre kyne	3 .0.0*d*
Thre horses	1 .0.0*d*
Thre store pygges	10.0*d*
The chroppe on the ground	4 .0.0*d*
One ironbound carte	1 .0.0*d*
horse gere ploughe and ploughgere	6.8*d*
Two podes of woode and 2 hovels	16.0*d*
Thre hennes and 2 ducks	1.8*d*
	£14.9.0*d*

2. John Robyns, carpenter of Ambridge, taken 1 May, 1586 by William Forrest, John Coxe and Simon Bartlett.

One cow	1 .6.8*d*
Two brass pottes	6.8*d*
One platter a sauser and sault and a candlestick	1.6*d*
One payer of blanketes 2 payers of sheetes one coverlett one bedsted one bolster	13.4*d*
A table bord and a furme	2.0*d*
Boordes and tymber	8.0*d*
His axe and other toles belonging to a carpentere	6.0*d*
Half a quarter of barley	4.0*d*
His apparayle	5.0*d*
	£3.13.2*d*

18

Cannybals and Cavallaers

In September 1642, soon after the outbreak of the Civil War, soldiers from the parliamentary army of 'cannybals-in-arms' fought a brief engagement with royalists at Hassett Bridge. Over three years later, in March 1646, when parliament was on the point of triumph, the king's last army – a few hundred Welsh levies under Sir Jacob Astley – toiled along the high road from Borchester to Hollerton, two days before their defeat at Stow-on-the-Wold.

In between, for three and a half years, the Great Rebellion passed Ambridge by. There is a story in *Borsetshire Recollected* of a cottager who was told of a parliamentary victory in 1644 (presumably Marston Moor) and replied: 'What, is they and the king still a-quarrelling then?' In an age when few could read, and it took a month for the *Mercurius Britanicus* news-sheet to reach Borchester from London, such ignorance cannot have been uncommon. The state of the harvest was a greater matter than the state of the nation.

The Lawson-Hope account-books show that on 3 September 1642, Thomas Lawson, Esquire departed to Nottingham, where his sovereign had raised the royal standard, and took with him two of his tenants, a Blower and a Gabriel. We should not assume from this rather unimpressive turn-out that Ambridge was lacking in loyalty to the king (although Penny Hassett certainly was, and remained so throughout the conflict). It is more likely that Ambridge folk were preoccupied with an immediate concern: the need to save as much corn from the fields as possible after the disastrous storm that swept the Midland counties on 27 August (noted in *Agricultural Records* by J.M. Stratton). The price of wheat was rising, from 44s 8d a quarter to 60s 2d a quarter in two years.

Thomas Lawson, Esquire and his two tenants followed the king to Nottingham, then across to the Welsh marshes and north to Shrewsbury. In the meantime, in London, Parliament ordered the Earl of Essex to 'march, with such forces as he saw fit, towards the army raised in his Majesty's name against the parliament and the kingdom.'

On 27 September that army marched into Borsetshire and billeted itself on Churcham. A day later it passed through Layton Cross and

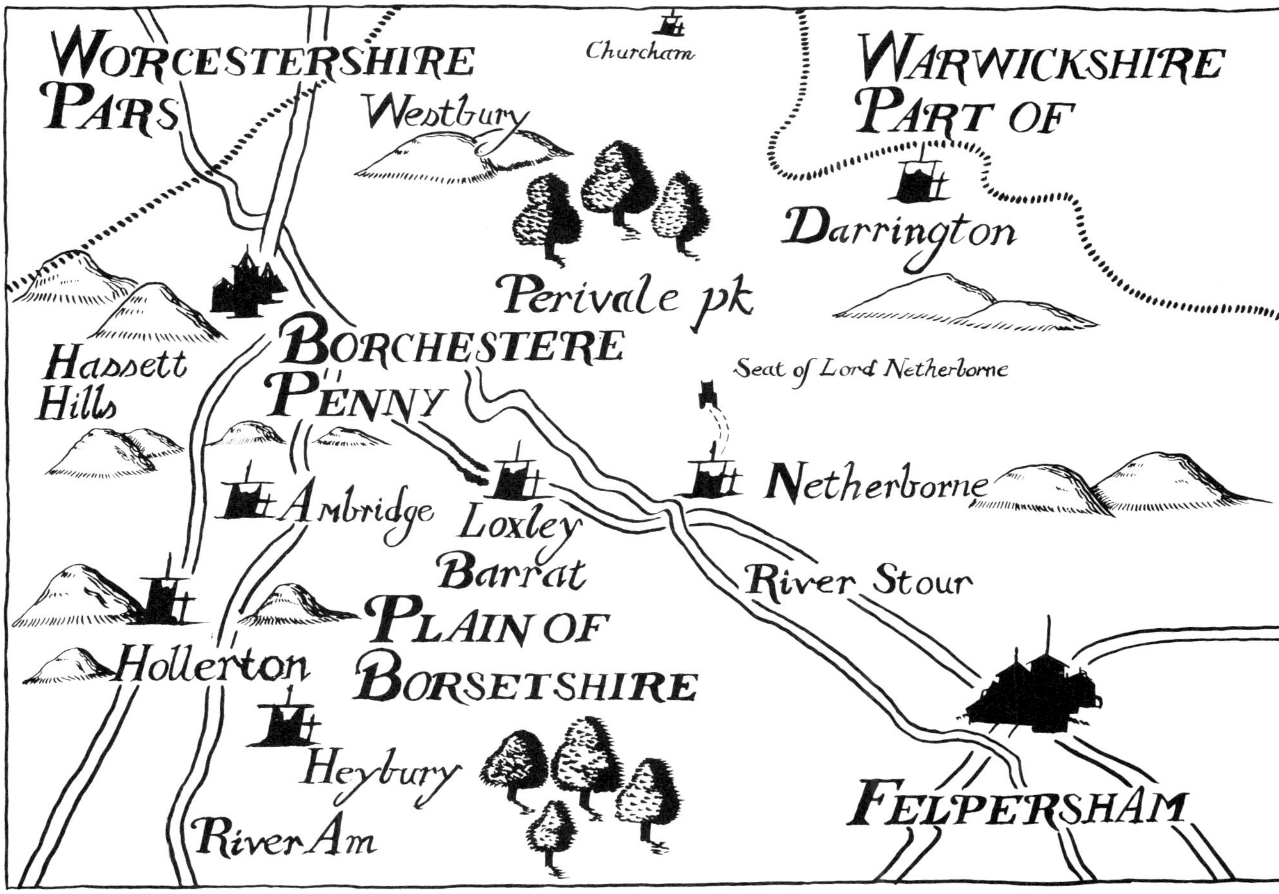

Part of Borsetshire in 1621.

reached Borchester in the evening. The army itself has been described by C.V. Wedgewood in *The King's War:*

His troops were undisciplined, untrained and greedy for plunder. Little attempt had been made to organize them into regiments. Captains and companies acted independently and the confusion was great.

There is no record of any troops entering Ambridge on 27 September (indeed, their road would have carried them a good ten miles to the east), but the village is dramatically mentioned in an account of the engagement at Hassett Bridge, which took place the following morning. It was written by a Londoner, Nehemiah Cook, and published in 1853 in the transactions of the Borsetshire Records Society under the title *Letters from a Subaltern Officer of the Earl of Essex's Army.*

Monday morninge wee marched out of Warwick-shere with aboute three hundred foote and a hundred horse until we came after two days to Borchestere. This is a very malignant towne. We pillaged the minister and tooke from him a drum and severall armes. This night our soildiers quartered themselves about the towne for foode and lodginge, but before we could eate or drinke an alarum cryed, 'Arme, arme, for the enemie is commenge', and in halfe an hower all our soildiers were cannybals in armes cryinge out for a dish of Cavallaers to supper, but the enemy came not, wherupon our soildiers cryed out to have a breakefast of Cavallaers.

In the morninge early our enemise consistinge of about two hundred horse and three hundred foote with ordinance led by the earle of Northampton, the Lord of Carnarvan, and the Lord Compton and Captn Legge, intended to set upon us before wee could gather our companies together, wee went to meete them with a few troopes of horse and sixe feild peeces, and being on fier to be at them wee marched throrow the corne and got the hill of them, wherupon they played upon us with their ordinances, but they came short. Our gunner tooke their owne bullet, sent it to them againe, and killed a horse and a man, wherupon all their foote companies fled and offered ther armes in Hollerton and Hassett for twelve pence a peece. Ther troopes whelinge about toke up ther dead bodies, but the horse they left behind, some of them having their guts beaten out on both sides. One drumner beinge dead at the bottome of the hill our knap sack boyes rifled to the shirt, which was very lowzy. Another drumner wee found in the inn at Ambrige, with his arme shot off, and lay a dieinge.

The mention of a royalist drummer boy dying in the Bull is curious. There is a persistent rumour of a ghost that makes tapping noises in an upstairs room – perhaps the 'tapping' is really the beat of a ghostly drum.

In autumn 1980 the survey team followed the route of the parliamentary forces (as confidently as Nehemiah Cook's description would allow) from Borchester south to Hassett Bridge, and carried out a methodical search of the hillside where the 'battle' was supposedly fought. The harvest was just over and long lines of straw waited to be either baled or burned. The Am is now hidden by trees, planted as cover for partridge in the mid-eighteenth century, and the modern buildings of Babylon Farm stand by the old Hollerton Road, which is no more than a sunken track (classified by Borsetshire County Council as a bridleway).

Nothing was found by the survey team, and although this was hardly surprising, it is more than possible that Nehemiah exaggerated the importance of the engagement, and that the *Victoria County History* gives a more accurate account:

Lord Compton attempted to hold the bridge at Hassett but was dislodged when the parliamentarians placed a field piece on the north slope of Plaiter's Hill and fired on the royalist position. The bridge had little strategic value, there being several places nearby where the Am was easily fordable after the dry summer.

The only relic of the Civil War found in Ambridge is a stone cannonball, discovered many years ago in the roots of a dead laurel bush by Walter Gabriel, who has used it ever since as a door-stopper. (It is currently on loan to the Ambridge Exhibition at Home Farm.) How long it had been in the bush it is hard to say; laurels were believed

Hassett Hill, looking down on Babylon Farm. The River Am is hidden behind the belt of trees. From here the Earl of Essex's men fired their field piece at the defenders of Hassett Bridge.

locally to ward off evil, and never disturbed unless completely dead. The survey team found eight laurels growing close to cottage doors and five of the occupiers knew it was 'unlucky' to interfere with them.

In St Stephen's Church, the incumbent, the Reverend Timothy Collyer, a royalist, was dispossessed in 1652 and the puritan Obadiah Norton put in his place. In 1660 the Reverend Collyer returned and dispossessed Norton.

The carved pew ends are reputed to have been taken from the church and hidden during the rebellion. The painted plaster roof of the nave was whitewashed over at this time, and has still to be fully restored. A section cleaned in the eighteen seventies shows a deep blue background covered in gold stars.

The fortunes of the Lawson family are referred to in several contemporary documents. Thomas Lawson was one of the tax commissioners who took the Borsetshire tax-gathering for August 1644 to the king at Oxford. In 1649 he 'compounded' with parliament and was allowed to retain his estate. The cost was heavy – four thousand pounds – and the family never recovered from the blow. The restoration of Charles II brought no financial recompense (only a gilt-framed etching of the monarch) and the estate was mortgaged twice over by 1689 when John Lawson saved the situation by marrying Annabel Hope, the elder daughter of a prosperous Bristol merchant.

19

The Eternal Round

For a thousand years the life of a cottager in Ambridge hardly changed. Long hours were worked on the land, with the ox and plough the only mechanical aids. Food was poor in quality and often scarce. After the Black Death, when the shortage of labourers for a brief time gave them the upper-hand in society, Piers Plowman marvelled at their temerity in refusing to 'dine a-day on worts (beans) a night old' and rejecting meat unless it 'be fresh flesh or fish fried or baked'. Between Saxon England and the 1850s there can have been few years when the Ambridge cottager had anything much better than rye bread and beans on his dinner table, and the price of corn, for century after century, was the only price that really mattered. Improvement was slow and undramatic. The Saxon labourer simply went to bed when darkness fell, the Tudor labourer perhaps had a tallow dip, and the early Victorian labourer an oil lamp. (The Ambridge name for nightfall, by the way, is 'daygate' and is still used by at least two of its older inhabitants.) The village was a self-contained, self-reliant community, looking to the weather for its prosperity, and to itself for its entertainment. There developed from this a rich circle of traditions based on the changing seasons; ploughing and harvest, fair and festival – an eternal round of village life that endured for hundreds of years, and is now almost gone.

We should not be too regretful, or sentimental, about this. The people who bemoan the death of village culture and folk-traditions are often the same people who complain about the withdrawal of rural bus services – not realizing that it was the introduction of the motor bus, and the wireless, in the thirties, that accelerated the decline of the old village life. What follows is an account of the 'Ambridge Year' as it is still remembered. It is culturally richer than anything that stems from the village now (bingo is played in the village hall, and there are country and western music nights at the Bull), but it was paid for with a thousand years of poverty, hunger and isolation. As late as the nineteenth century infant mortality was high, and even in Tudor times few people lived beyond their forties. Superstitions that seem quaint and interesting now had a terrible power when man feared the dark-

ness, and death was always close at hand.

The Ambridge Year is, nevertheless, a triumph; the voice of the common people of England.

The first bus service to Ambridge started in 1904 and was run by the Borchester and District Motor Omnibus Co.

January

Until late in the nineteenth century Ambridge boys maintained the noisy custom of letting in the New Year by going from house to house and banging on the doors with sticks. 'Noisy urchins roam at will from midnight till the dawn of day, and no peace is to be obtained,' complained the Vicar of Ambridge, the Reverend Truelove, in 1874. On their progress round the village the boys sang:

We wish you a merry Christmas and a happy New Year;
A pocket of money, and a cellar of beer;
A fat pig to serve you throughout the long year.

They then cracked their sticks together and shouted:

Open the door, let the New Year in,
Or we'll clatter our sticks and make a din!

Back Lane, Ambridge, 1886.

Superstitions connected with the New Year are remembered by Sammy Whipple, the shepherd at Home Farm:

For a start, nobody was ever supposed to pay their debts or bills on New Year's Day or else they'd have a trail of debts following them all year through. Nothing had to be taken out of the house – nothing at all – but you had to get as many things as possible into it, new things that is. The worst luck was for a woman to be the first over the door after midnight. My goodness, that brought bad luck with it. Some old ladies in Back Lane used to pay a little dark-haired lad sixpence to come round first thing New Year's Day with a piece of coal, and one year he forgot and there the old dears were, leaning out of the window, begging for any man to cross the threshold. Some folk used to put money out on New Year's Eve – just a few pennies – out on the back windowsill, and bring it back into the house after midnight. It was a question of bringing luck and fortune in, you see. Men and money, but not women.

Borsetshire had its equivalent of the Coventry 'God Cakes' on New Year's Day – triangular-shaped pastry-cases filled with a kind of mincemeat – which were still being sold on the streets in Borchester up to the start of the First World War.

January prophesies include:

January Spring
Not worth a pin.

In January if sun appear
March and April pay full dear.

January's floods
Never boded husbandman good.

Ploughing with oxen. The horse would soon take over from the ox and two horses would be expected to pull a single furrow plough. The 'ploughboy' at the head of the team was generally a schoolboy (playing truant, as he would at haymaking and harvest) who turned the leading ox at the end of each furrow.

Ambridge experts clearly mistrusted warm weather and rain in January, but another rhyme makes it plain what was looked for: cold, dry weather, with the land good for sowing.

Who in January sows oats
May hope to gather golden groats.

Plough Monday – the first Monday after Twelfth Night – is the official start of the farming year and is still celebrated in Penny Hassett, where a plough decorated with green and yellow ribbons (representing grass and corn) is drawn through the village street, and money collected for a Borchester charity.

February

In the Borchester area Candlemas Day (2 February) was the traditional day for cock-fighting and drinking mulled ale and to celebrate the end of winter. It was also an important day for weather forecasters:

If Candlemas Day be fair and bright
Winter will have another flight
But if Candlemas Day be wind and rain
Winter be gone and won't come again.

Another rhyme recalled by Tom Forrest confirms that good weather was considered a warning of storms to come, when the farmer would need extra forage for his livestock:

Warm and sunny on Candlemas Day
Saddle your horse and go buy hay.

Other weather lore known locally includes the famous:

February fills the dyke
Either with the black or white
But if with white, the better to like.

Meaning that snow, giving the seed a nice warm insulation, is better than rain flooding the seedbed. Another saying: 'Fog in February, Frost in May' is still widely believed, and might well have some basis in fact. Certainly local fruit farmers take careful note of the number of foggy nights early in the year.

Almost every child who attended Ambridge primary school in the fifties can remember the seasonal stories told by teacher Elsie Catcher, who was a keen collector of traditional children's tales. In February she always told the story of the origin of the snowdrop, recalled here by Shula Archer:

When Adam and Eve were turned out of the Garden of Eden it was the middle of winter, and they nearly froze to death before Adam managed to find a cave, and kill some wild animals for them to eat. He was content then, but Eve wept for the beautiful flowers she had left behind in the Garden of Eden, and one day she went back, only to be turned away at the gate by an angel dressed in gold. Again Eve wept bitterly, and as she turned away the angel took pity on her. He caught a snowflake as it drifted down, and when he breathed on it gently it came to life and blossomed like a flower. The angel then gave it to Eve and told her to take comfort in the thought that spring and summer were coming.

Shrove Monday was known as Pease Monday in Waterley Cross (an eccentric squire's wife in the eighteenth century used to dole out pea soup to the villagers) and on Shrove Tuesday the village boys of Ambridge were out again with their sticks:

Nick, stick, stone
Give us a pancake and we'll go home.

In Hollerton, boys marked St Valentine's Day by singing for apples, which they then fried as fritters.

Good Morrow Valentine
First it's yours and then it's mine.
Please give I a Valentine.

March

There is a tradition that on 1 March Ambridge housewives used to get up early to sweep the fleas from the doorstep. (This custom is also known in places as far apart as Cornwall and Carmarthen.) Much folklore for March has to do with medicines and cures, for at the end of the winter the old and the ill were at their weakest and generally suffering

Marshmarigolds growing alongside the River Am in spring.

from a considerable vitamin deficiency. Ambridge's forefathers may not have known about vitamins, but they did know about green vegetables:

Eat leeks in March, and garlic in May
All the year after, doctors may play.

If they would in March drink nettles always
So many fair maidens wouldn't go to the clay.

Joe Grundy marks St David's Day every year by recounting the story told to him by his grandfather. The Welsh (he says) were once invaded by ferocious monkeys and asked the English to kill them but the English couldn't tell the monkeys and the Welsh apart and killed both until the Welsh started wearing leeks in their caps as a distinguishing mark. This story is clearly the remnant of an old antagonism and a reminder that Borsetshire was at one time almost part of the Welsh marches, suffering from repeated raiding parties before Edward I's reign.

Mothering Sunday (the fourth in Lent) generally falls in March, and the Borsetshire custom is for grown-up children, married and unmarried, to visit their mothers.

The lad and lass on Mothering Day
Hie home to their mother so dear.
'Tis a kiss for she and a kiss for they,
A chine of pork and sprig of bay,
A song and dance but never a tear.

As well as roast pork, the traditional food to eat was frumenty – wheat boiled with raisins – and Borchester shops used to sell specially prepared bags of wheat, in which the husk had been separated from the grain.

Local weather lore for March includes:

March damp and warm
Does farmer much harm.

March showers
Make no summer bowers.

These confirm the old proverb that 'a peck of March dust is worth a king's ransom'. Farmers then as now need dry weather to break down the soil and drill their spring barley.

April

Sammy Whipple has spent most of his life working with livestock – first sheep, and more recently cows and calves in the new multi-suckling unit at Home Farm. His father, however, was a ploughman and swore by the following:

When the elmen leaf is as big as a mouse's ear
Then to sow barley never fear.

When the elmen leaf is as big as an ox's eye
Then says I, 'Hie, boys! Hie!'
When elm leaves are as big as a shilling
Plant kidney beans, if to plant 'em you're willing.
When elm leaves are as big as a penny
You must plant beans if you mean to have any.

All Fool's Day was celebrated, as elsewhere, by the playing of tricks and Dan Archer can remember as a boy being sent to the village shop to ask for 'a penn'orth of pigeon's milk'.

There's a local belief that anyone who gets up early on Easter morning and climbs Lakey Hill will see the sun dance. Easter Day in Penny Hassett meant, for the girls, some new clothes and for the boys an attempt to catch a hare. If they took it to the parson before ten o'clock he had to give them fifty eggs and a groat (fourpence). And in Borchester, Easter Monday and Tuesday were known as 'heaving days'. On the Monday men lifted women into their arms and kissed them, and on the Tuesday the situation was reversed. A report in the *Borchester Echo* for April 1885 says:

> Passing through streets inhabited by working people on Tuesday last, groups of jolly matrons could be observed seated round wooden tables on which stood foaming tankards of ale. Woe the luckless man who ventured too close to their sovereignty! As soon as he passed them he was pursued – and as sure as he was pursued he was taken – and as sure as he was taken he was heaved and kissed, and compelled to pay fourpence for leave to depart.

Heaving was not peculiar to Borchester, but was common in Birmingham and several Warwickshire villages, including Avon Dassett in the far south of the county.

The 'Riding of St George' is still observed in Felpersham on 23 April, when a man representing England's patron saint rides through the town followed by a 'dragon' (in this case a charity-float organized by Felpersham Round Table). The custom was once shared with Stratford-on-Avon, which now devotes 23 April to a celebration of Shakespeare's birthday.

May

Doris Archer, who died in her eighty-first year, having lived in Ambridge all her life, was fond of quoting a rhyme from her childhood days about the 'magical' hawthorn dew to be found on Lakey Hill:

That fair maid
  Who at break of day
Climbs Lakey Hill
  On the first of May
And washes in dew
  From the hawthorn tree
Shall ever afterwards
  Beautiful be.

Morris dancers outside the Bull, 1890.

The girl was supposed to shake the dew from the hawthorn blossom (there is still a hawthorn hedge on Lakey Hill, dividing Willow Farm from what is now Ambridge Farmers Ltd) and bathe her face with it exactly as the sun rose over Leader's Wood.

May Day itself has not been celebrated in the village for over sixty years, and the permanent maypole, if it ever existed, has long since gone. May Day customs have been revived recently, however, largely because of the new May public holiday. Strangely enough, the sight of children dancing round the maypole a couple of years ago brought criticism from some older inhabitants of Ambridge, who could remember when the village celebrated on 12 May – 'Old May Day'. Tom Forrest believes the last celebration was during the First World War, when he was seven or eight years old.

It wasn't a regular maypole, more a sort of tower, about eight foot high, and made out of twigs covered in leaves. I believe it was also called a Jack-in-the-

Green. Anyway, us children had to go round the farms and cottages asking for stuff to deck it out – ribbons and suchlike. I remember howling my head off but Doris still dragged me round behind her – I was that much younger I couldn't well say no. I reckon Doris had been told to get the maypole rigged out by Lettie Lawson-Hope, the squire's wife. Doris was in service then, you see, and she only had one afternoon a fortnight off, so I can't imagine she'd have wanted to mess about with decking maypoles, not without having been told to do it. Anyway, it was a nice afternoon in the end, with buns to eat, and the bloke inside the maypole – or Jack-in-the-Green – swayed his arms about covered in twigs, and we all had to dance round him while a fiddler played a particular tune over and over.

As with May Day revelries, morris dancing has undergone a revival in Borsetshire in recent years. In 1904 the *Borchester Echo* remarked sadly that 'the art of the morris is dead, and its secrets lost', but in 1980 there were four villages in the Ambridge area with their own morris-men. Those from Heybury visit the Bull at least twice a year, and perform the traditional dances representing Robin Hood, Little John and Maid Marion. In the eighteenth century May Day was also known as Robin Hood's Day, and Tom Forrest has, in his collection of country folk songs, one which used to be sung locally when he was a boy:

Robin Hood and Little John, they both are gone to fair O
And we will to the merry greenwood to see what they do there O
And for the chase of the buck and doe
And to fetch the summer home O
For summer is acome again and winter it is gone O.

There is no record of Oak Apple Day (29 May) being celebrated with special events in Ambridge, though it is certain that schoolchildren must have worn oak leaves, as in other parts of England, to mark the escape of Charles II from the roundheads after Worcester Fight. Until the First World War draysmen from Shire's Brewery, Borchester, decorated their horses' heads and their own hats with sprigs of oak.

May was always considered an unhealthy and unlucky month, and the weather could never please Ambridge folk. 'A hot May makes for a fat churchyard' is still commonly quoted, and Joe Grundy knows the rhyme:

He who bathes in May
Will soon be laid in clay.

June

If the weather in May was never right, in June it was never wrong, at least if the rhymes recalled by Dan Archer are anything to go by.

June damp and warm
Does the farmer no harm.

Sammy Whipple, shepherd at Home Farm, seen here as a boy on the Ambridge estate. The machine which turned the shearing knives had to be turned laboriously by hand, and the knives themselves were much narrower than those used today.

A dripping June
Puts the world in tune.

A dry June
Brings the harvest good and soon.

But before the harvest of hay or corn, there was the sheep shearing – hard, back-breaking work before the days of motor-powered shears. At Home Farm, Sammy Whipple remembers the feasts that were held in the farm kitchen when the job was completed.

It was always a greasy sort of do. You could wash your hands under the pump, but you couldn't get the grease off your clothes, not after handling all them sheep. Every man's trousers were thick with it, lanolin off the wool, and very good for the skin, but very smelly when you had ten or fifteen of you in there on a hot afternoon with more than a few flies buzzing about, and the old stove nearly red hot from boiling up pieces of beef and onions and tatties. The boss always made the same remarks:

Here's health to the flock
May God increase the stock
Twenty where there's ten
May we all come here
Sheep shearing again.

But most of us felt we were sick to death of sheep just for the moment. It was always the same. Beef and onions, and a Christmas pudding specially saved from the year before. Nowadays we get a shearing gang in – two or three blokes, New Zealanders likely as not – and the boss gives them a few glasses of beer by the swimming pool.

Until the late nineteenth century, Ambridge folk used to 'beat the bounds' in early June, a custom that is still followed in several Midland villages. It must have been a curious combination of religion and tomfoolery, with the parson and churchwardens marking the parish boundary and numerous small boys coming behind and 'bumping' each other on the ground. The parson read from the gospels at certain points and there is still a 'gospel oak' standing on the old Hollerton to Borchester turnpike where it crosses the Ambridge parish boundary.

Midsummer's Eve was always one of the most magical nights of the country year, when young girls could sit in the church porch at midnight (after fasting all day) and see the form of the man they would marry, and farmers could protect their crops from evil spells by lighting bonfires and marching round the fields with flaming torches. Dan Archer remembers a communal bonfire which was lit on Lakey Hill when he was young:

They always said it was to charm away witches and save the crops. It's a nailbiting time, is June, watching the corn and worrying about diseases and aphids and what have you. Nowadays you can spray against just about everything except drought, or get some bloke in a light aeroplane to do it for you, a thirty-acre field in about ten minutes. It was different then, though, and folk had a lot more faith in superstitions – walking round each field in turn, holding

Glebe Cottage.

up a burning brand, and saying certain special words. I never saw it happen, mind, and I haven't any idea what they said. By the time I came back to the village after the First War everything was changing. We had a bonfire on Lakey Hill and burnt an effigy of a witch on it every year, but it was just a bit of fun for the lads and the girls in the village.

It's a wonder to me how any of us had the energy in the middle of haymaking, but we kept the custom going for five or six years. It was after the bonfire in 1918 that I started courting Doris. She was working at the Manor House and I daresay she was supposed to be tucked up in bed on Midsummer's Eve, but there she was on Lakey Hill with two other maids, all sharing a mug of cider and laughing away. I can see her now, standing in the light from the fire, watching the witch burn and holding a flower in her hand – a sprig of St John's wort. You know what a lovely yellow flower it's got, and it's always at its best round midsummer. Anyway, I made some joke about only daftheads picking flowers in the middle of the night, and she turned pink and the other two giggled fit to bust. I only found out afterwards that if a girl plucked a sprig of St John's wort on Midsummer's Eve and kept it in a hankie till Christmas, then wore it in her bosom, her future husband would come and take it from her. That was the story. Next year, though, when I reminded her about it and asked if she'd still got it tucked down her blouse, she told me not to be cheeky and denied ever having had a sprig of it in the first place. I told her she'd better not let anybody take it from her but me, and soon after that we got engaged to be married. It's certainly funny stuff, though, St John's wort. Folk used to hang a sprig of it over their cottage doors to ward off evil spirits, and Walter Gabriel's grandmother made all sorts of potions and lotions out of it. Her cottage was a marvellous place when I was a lad, full of jars of badger fat and all sorts of country cures. She used the flower of St John's wort to make a throat gargle, and a sort of ointment out of its leaves.

Another thing about Midsummer's Day. You'll never hear the cuckoo after that. He's still here, of course, stays till August, but he doesn't call out after midsummer. That's what they always said, and I've never heard one, so it might have some truth in it.

July

The Ambridge Sick and Provident Society held its club day in July throughout late Victorian times, but this was the only social event to take place during one of the busiest farming months. A *Borchester Echo* report in 1888 says that there was a special service preached in St Stephen's Church in the morning, and that was followed by the Club Dinner. Curiously enough, villagers did not gather in one place, but each family was given a hot meat pie and a spiced raisin pudding from the village bakery and then sent home to eat it. During the afternoon there were games on the village green. It was a day when folk who had left the village were traditionally supposed to come back to see their families and friends.

St Swithin's Day falls on 15 July and all the world knows that on 'St Swithin's Day, if thous doest rain, For forty days it will remain'. In Ambridge and villages extenting to the vale of Evesham and Worcestershire, however, rain is looked for and welcomed as a help to the fruit harvest. 'St Swithin is christening the little apples' is a well-known local saying.

The houseleek is in flower in July and at one time Borsetshire villagers used to grow the plant on the roofs of their houses, believing that it protected them against thunderstorms. The juice extracted from the thick, fleshy stems of the houseleek is an old Ambridge cure for a sore throat, and the stems are rubbed on nettle-stings in preference to the dock leaf.

The poppy is in flower also, and there is a local belief that the poppy springs from ground where blood has been shed. There are certainly masses of them along the borders of the hayfield where royalists and roundheads fought briefly for possession of Hassett Bridge.

August

'As merry as the first of August' is a Borsetshire saying which has its roots buried in the distant past, when Lammas Day (from the Saxon *Hlaf-mass,* meaning feast of bread) was celebrated with ritual feasting; and before then, in pagan times, when the first of the grain was offered to the Gods in the hope of good weather for the rest of the harvest.

The Penny Hassett 'Revel' takes place on Old Lammas Day (13 August) and is a curious festival that can be traced back to the Middle Ages. The central figure is the Queen of the Revel, a village girl of

Harvesting with oxen. The beasts in this picture are very thin, with hardly any hind quarters at all. Borsetshire still used the ox as a beast of burden long after farmers in neighbouring counties had gone over to the horse and started raising their bullocks for beef cattle.

about thirteen, who has six attendants dressed in white and blue. Wrestling, dancing and games take place during the afternoon. The Revel has traditionally been sneered at by Ambridge people, who say the folk of Penny Hassett are so slow they celebrate May Day three months late. More local rivalry is reflected in the rhyme:

The Hassett boys are very good boys
  The Hollerton boys are better,
The Ambridge boys can stand on one leg
  And kick them in the gutter.

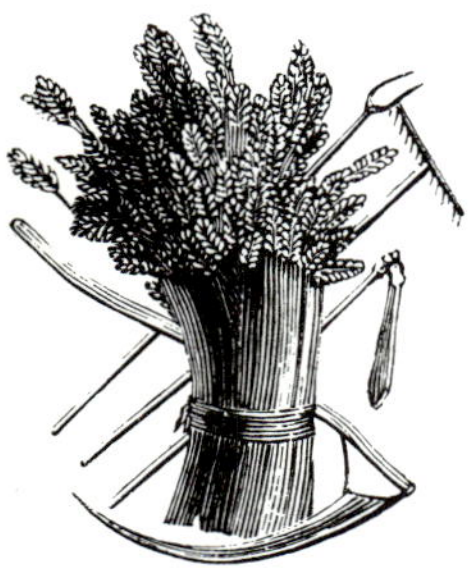

The August corn harvest is the crown of the farming year. When the last load was collected from the fields Ambridge farmers used to decorate the wagon with ribbons and flowers, and at the farm the labourers were treated to cakes and ale. A day or two later there would be the harvest home, with food similar to that served at the sheep-shearing feast – boiled beef and onions, plum pudding and ale, with bread baked in the shape of an ear of wheat. Nowadays the Parish Council organizes a communal harvest home in the village hall (in 1980 the supper was cold ham, jacket potatoes, tomato salad and lemon meringue pie) but until the early nineteen-twenties each farm provided its own celebration for its own workers. At Brookfield Simon Cooper could remember, when he started on the farm as a boy, the foreman reciting at the harvest-supper:

Here's a health unto our master, the founder of the feast
I hope to God in Heaven, his soul may be at rest.
That all things may prosper, whate'er he takes in hand,
For we are all his servants, and all at his command.
So drink, boys, drink, and see you do not spill,
For if you do you shall drink two,
For it is our master's will.

The ale flowed, the fiddler played, and there was beef and pudding in plenty. But Ambridge tradition also shows another side to the harvest, the spectre of poverty and starvation that led – on one occasion at least – to men being clubbed and beaten. Dan Archer was told the story by his father, John.

It was in eighteen sixty – and that's a year nobody who was brought up round here has ever been able to forget. All my life, when there's been a poor haymaking or corn harvest, folk have said, 'It's nearly as bad as eighteen sixty.' Mind you, I don't suppose Brian Aldridge or Mike Tucker or even young Tony at Bridge Farm would know what it meant. It's the older people I'm talking about. My Dad told the tale of eighteen sixty every New Year's Eve, sitting hunched over the fire in the parlour at Brookfield. All about how spring was wet – the wettest for hundreds of years, and then it rained all through June and the haymaking was the worst in living memory. When it came to the corn harvest, it had been so cold there wasn't any sprouting corn at all. They were still trying to harvest wheat in October – and barley. Root crops failed com-

Brookfield Farm, looking east down the Vale of Am, showing where fox cubs have lain out among the ripening wheat.

pletely and there was sheep rot everywhere. The trouble started over the hill at Babylon Farm – a man called Ball had the place, and he must have been a rough customer. Anyway, he'd harvested what he could – which wasn't much – when the parson's men came into the field to take the tythe. They always went into the field once the corn was cut and piled in shucks, and they took away one shuck in ten. It was a bitter thing for the farm to have to watch when the harvest was bad and the price of corn was going to be sky-high. On this occasion the parson's men tried to take one more shuck than they ought to have done and Farmer Ball and his men gave them such a beating they didn't recover for six months. The Balls didn't come to church after that – folk used to say they'd been excommunicated, but of course they hadn't been.

Those must have been desperate times for poor folk. Nearly every labourer's wife and children used to go out gleaning after the harvest. The church bell used to be rung every morning to tell the gleaners that they could start – so nobody had an unfair advantage. People were so poor they'd have been out there in the middle of the night otherwise. Anyway, the churchwarden had to ring the bell, then stand at the gate and announce which fields were ready for gleaning. It wouldn't mean much now, I don't suppose. Madmore Meadow, Rattler's Piece, Rush Furrows – they're all fields up at Brookfield. The churchwarden would read them out and the gleaners'd be off with their bags and baskets. If a farmer hadn't quite finished with a field he'd leave one swathe uncut to tell the gleaners to keep out. On the first day of gleaning the women were supposed to wear clean petticoats, and they'd put the first day's corn in a pile in the bedroom – that brought luck and good food for the coming year. It's hard to realize it, but after a year like eighteen sixty some people must have nearly starved.

Pig-roasting at Borchester Fair.

September

The last full moon before the autumn equinox on 21 September is traditionally known as the Harvest Moon because its light enabled harvesters to work late into the night. Michaelmas Day, 29 September, marks the end of the farming year and was a date of some significance in the days when labourers were hired from one Michaelmas to the next and had then to seek new jobs. Borchester's hiring fair (sometimes called the mop because maidservants looking for work used to display minature mops in their caps) is still held on the first Thursday after Michaelmas. Nowadays you can buy anything from cheap saucepans and jeans to hot-dogs and candyfloss, and spend hours on the dodgems or sideshows, but nobody expects to see farmworkers and maid-servants looking for work. Tom Forrest remembers an old Borsetshire folksong which illustrates the bargaining procedure which used to take place a hundred years ago:

Farmer: Come all you lads that be here for service,
Come here you jolly dogs.
Who will help me with my harvest,
Milk my cows and feed my hogs?
Yonder stands a likely fellow
As e'er trod in leathern shoe.
Cans't though plough and cans't thou harrow?
Servant: Oh yes master! And I can milk too.
Farmer: Here's five pounds in standing wages.
Daily well thou shalt be fed.
With good cabbage, beef and bacon,
Butter milk and oaten bread.

October

At the end of September, according to Walter Gabriel, 'the devil was kicked out of heaven by St Michael and managed to show a last bit of spite by spitting on a blackberry bush before he fell down into Hell.' There is a widespread belief throughout Borsetshire that blackberries are useless after Michaelmas Day – eaten raw they will cause indigestion, and jam or jelly made with them will never set.

A candle auction used to be held in mid-October at the Bull, not to sell candles but to auction grazing rights on a dozen or so pieces of roadside land in the parish. A small piece of candle, perhaps a quarter of an inch long, was lit, and the highest price bid for each piece of land when the candle went out was accepted.

The feast of St Simon and St Jude on 28 October provided yet another opportunity for Ambridge maidens to discover who they would marry. This time it was necessary to peel an apple so that the peel came off in one long strip, and recite:

St Simon and St Jude,
  On you I intrude,
By this paring I hold to discover,
  Without any delay
I pray you today
  To tell me the name of my lover.

She then had to throw the peel over her left shoulder, and if the spell worked it would lie on the ground in the shape of her future partner's first name initial. If this failed, the desperate maiden had to wait until Halloween, when she could sit in her bedroom in front of a mirror, eating an apple and brushing her hair by the light of a candle. If she was destined to be married at all, the face of her future husband would appear.

Jethro Larkin remembers his father telling him that on Halloween Night the images of the people who were going to die in the village during the next twelve months would pass through St Stephen's churchyard. If the procession was disturbed, the person who saw it would become a victim and be buried in the churchyard within a year.

November

Guy Fawkes night is still celebrated with the traditional bonfire on the village green, although this custom seems to be in the process of change, or at least modernization. Peggy Archer was one of the organizers in 1980:

> The astonishing thing was that I asked nearly every child present if they knew the traditional rhyme – you know, 'Always remember the fifth of November, gunpowder, treason and plot. I see no reason why gunpowder, treason should ever be forgot'. But hardly a child knew more than the first line.

The bonfire is well organized now. We had jacket potatoes cooked in the Aga at Home Farm (though some children still insisted on pushing potatoes into the fire and eating them half-raw and covered in ash) and my son-in-law Brian brought them down in his Range Rover – we sold them for fifteen pence each in aid of a children's charity. Then there was a disco dance organized by Jennifer in the village hall. Next year I hope we'll be able to stop people bringing their own fireworks, which is always dangerous, and charge for a properly organized firework display. The trouble is that when they tried it at Penny Hassett they had a lot of men on motorbikes turn up who just roared about and refused to pay.

11 November is St Martin's Day and now passes almost unnoticed in Ambridge. In medieval times, however, Martinmas was known as the killing time, when most of the livestock (which could not be fed through the winter) was killed and salted. At the Martinmas Feast, villagers ate their last fresh meat for many months.

The weather is often good – known as St Martin's Little Summer – and Joe Grundy says that over the years he has come to believe one piece of weather lore:

Ice before Martinmas enough to bear a duck,
The rest of the winter is sure to be but muck.

In the nineteenth century, children in Waterley Cross marked St Clement's Day (23 November) by going from cottage to cottage in search of presents. Their traditional song was recorded in *Borsetshire Byways*.

Clemeny, Clemeny, Clemeny mine!
A good red apple and a pint of wine.
Some of your mutton and some of your veal,
If it is good, pray give a deal.
If it is not, pray give some salt.
Clement comes but once a year
Off with the pot, and on with the pan
A good red apple and I'll begin.

December

At Edgeley Manor, a yule log was always drawn to the house by a horse on Christmas Eve, and having been lit was not supposed to be allowed to go out during the twelve days of Christmas. There does not seem to be any other Christmas customs peculiar to the Ambridge area, although local songs include:

Welcome Christmas, which brings us all good cheer,
Pies and puddings, roast pork and strong beer.

and a song which was sung by carol singers before the First World War:

Our Wassail bowl is full with apples and spice
Grant to taste it once or twice
And joy come to our jolly Wassail.

It is believed in Ambridge, as elsewhere, that cattle kneel down in their stalls at midnight on Christmas Eve and that during the twelve days of Christmas there is great peace and freedom from evil. Bee-keepers also say that if they go out to their beehives on Christmas Eve they can hear the bees singing Christmas carols.

The traditional meet of the South Borsetshire hunt takes place outside the Feathers in Borchester on Boxing Day.

20

The Labourer and the Land

My board is simply spread,
I have a little food to spare
But thou shalt break my wholesome bread,
And have a wholesome share.
For while the faggot burns
To warm my cottage floor,
They never shall say the poor man turns
A poorer from his door.

On Plough Monday, the first Monday after the twelfth day of Christmas, the great plough was drawn through Ambridge by eight oxen, yoked in pairs on either side of the long plough pole (forty plough-poles by four made the traditional Borsetshire acre) and decorated with ribbands to celebrate the start of the farming year.

The oxen in the nineteenth century would toil for twelve years or so before being briefly fattened and sold as beef. The ploughman, in his sleeved waistcoat and corduroy trousers with leggings, worked for about twelve shillings a week, with an extra shilling if he tended his animals on Sundays and broke in new oxen for the team. (First the beast was yoked to a heavy log and turned loose to tire himself out. Then he had to be taught the basic directions – 'Au' to move nearer to the left side, 'Eet' to move nearer the right, 'Comming gen' to turn to the left side, and 'Gee gen' to turn to the right.)

Mowing involved everyone living on the farm. The picture shows a mower drawn by two horses, and behind that a horse rake which collected the hay into ridges after it had been turned by hand. Seven or eight people, men, women and children, would be required to turn the hay. The photograph was taken at Home Farm in about 1910.

Before the spring ploughing came the muck spreading, using dung from the byre and brought by the farmer from the privies (or 'bumbly-holes' as they were called) of Ambridge. The February air was full of acrid smoke and the smell of manure: fires smouldering in fields where 'twitch' or spear-grass had been ripped from the soil with harrows and was being burned.

After the ploughing came bean setting, with four beans being placed in each hole: 'One for the pigeon, one for the crow, one to perish and one to grow.' A labourer went first, making holes with his two steel-capped dibbers, and behind him came the women of the village with calico bags tied round their waists, dropping the seed into the holes. In Ambridge in 1880 they received a shilling a day.

The hours of a labourer depended on the time of year, the rise and set of the sun. As early as St Valentine's Day, Ambridge farmers would announce the coming of spring and from then on labourers worked from six in the morning until six at night. Village children also worked long hours. Joseph Arch, founder of the farmworkers' union, had his first job in his home village of Barford in Warwickshire, crow-scaring, for which he was paid fourpence a day. 'The day was a twelve-hour one,' he later recalled, 'and it sometimes happened that I got more than was in the bargain – and that was a smart taste of the farmer's stick when he ran across me outside the field I had been set to watch.'

Peas were sown broadcast, by a method that did not change from the sixteenth century to the nineteenth, and was described in the *Borsetshire Husbandman*:

You must not sow if the land synge or cry or make any noyse under thy fete. Put thy pees into thy hopper and take a brode thong of ledder or of garthe webbe of an ell longe, and fasten it to the endes of the hopper, and put it over thy head like a leyshe, and stande in the myddle of the lande where the sacke lyethe . . . and set thy left foote before, and take a handful of pees, and whan thou takest up thy right foote then caste thy pees from the alle abrode, and whan thy left foote repeth take an other handful, and so at every eleven paces . . . so that thy fote and hande agree, and than ye shal sowe even . . .

The corn was planted and harrowed, the field vegetables sown and the animals turned out to graze. The principal workers (or farm servants as they were known until late Victorian times) were the ploughman, shepherd, cowherd and oxherd. Before the land was enclosed the

The fiddle or seed-thrower.

Marney's Farm. In 1870 Joseph Marney raised a family of eight children and provided employment for his five sons and three labourers. The farm is now part of Ambridge Farmers Ltd and is used to house sheep-rearing equipment.

cowherd and oxherd would lead their cattle out to the field each day with a blast on their horn and from then until sunset they remained under their care.

Behind the Ambridge garage (which used to be the smithy) there still stands the remains of the huge grindstone where the men of the village used to sharpen their scythes in preparation for haymaking or corn harvest, and 'set' each tool by holding the tip of the blade against the toe of a boot, and then adjusting the handle until the balance was perfect.

In the hayfield a dozen men would work behind the foreman, mowing in a line, each man keeping the length of a scythe from the man in front. When the foreman was thirsty he would call a halt and pour beer into a single, enormous mug which would be handed to each man in turn. The foreman noted what beer was drunk and collected the money to pay for it. At the end of haymaking the squire gave each man a shilling bonus and each woman sixpence, and the gamekeeper provided a barrel of beer as a thank you to the haymakers for not disturbing sitting partridges.

The sight of corn being cut by men and scythes was soon to vanish as horse-drawn mowers came into use. It was a sight recalled vividly by countryman Michael Home:

> It was a superb morning of early August and as I came to the height of land and looked across the great field I saw something I shall never forget. In the near distance at least a score of men were mowing barley, the lord (foreman) at their head. There was the faint swish as the scythes met the standing corn and the steady, ceaseless rhythm of arms and bodies and scythes in unison. Each man was spaced regularly behind the man ahead and the young sun would catch the gleaming scythes as they swung, and in the labour of those score of men was an incredible beauty and an energy as of some relentless purpose.

The break for tea was the best part of the harvest day. Breakfast was snatched in the half light of dawn, and there was only half an hour allowed for dinner at eleven o'clock. But in the afternoon wives and small children came to the hayfield with cans of hot tea, cut bread and butter and cakes, and sat with the men. Even when the foreman gave the word for work to restart the women would sit talking and the children would play until dusk.

The corn harvest was the one time of the year when the labourer – who was generally employed by the week and could be laid off at any time – was able to make extra money. In Ambridge a deputation of labourers (forerunners of the union) met farmers and farm stewards in the upstairs room at the Bull and agreed a harvest rate, so much for each man, no matter how long the harvest took. If the work was completed in a fortnight the labourer could make four times his usual wage, but in a bad year he could be worse off than usual, and that meant disaster, because most labourer's families depended on the harvest bounty to pay back-rent and accumulated debts. The *Felpersham Evening Post* started publication in 1881 as a 'radical voice' and six months later published the average weekly outgoings of a labourer with a wife and four children.

Rent, including garden and pigsty	2.00*d*
Bread, 8 loaves	2.10*d*
Flour	9*d*
Meat, 6lb at 8*d* a pound (usually bacon)	4.00*d*
Potatoes	10*d*
Cheese, one lb at 8*d*	8*d*
Sugar, 2lb at 3*d*	6*d*
Tea, half a pound at 2*s*	1.00*d*
Butter, one lb at 1*s*	1.00*d*
Milk	1.00*d*
Treacle	3*d*
Salt and pepper	2*d*
Candles and paraffin	6*d*
Fuel	1.06*d*
Clothes, washing materials, etc	2.08*d*
Tools, furniture	10*d*
	£1.0.6*d*

The total (which took no account of beer money) was more than the average labourer could earn and families were only able to survive because at busy times of the farming year, with perhaps two sons and the wife working in the fields, the family as whole could double or treble its income. Other foods, too, were cheap in season: skimmed milk at a halfpenny for three or four pints and eggs a halfpenny each when hens were laying plentifully. The head and trimmings of a pig could be bought cheaply and boiled down to make 'pork cheese' or brawn.

Haymaking at Bull Farm, 1895. Bull Farm was unusual in being the only farm to use horses instead of oxen in the village.

The labourer's cottage generally had a small living-room and a kitchen-scullery, with two rooms above. The ceilings were rarely more than six foot in height. Families tended to be large, and tuberculosis and consumption common. Sanitation was primitive. The private privy was a luxury and in many cases groups of cottages had a movable wooden framework over a communal 'bumbly-hole'.

When the harvest was in and the stacks of cut wheat and barley thatched against threshing-time, the ritual of the year began again. Michaelmas brought the autumn dung-spreading and the clearing of stubble fields with the breast plough, which labourers pushed along the ground, slicing the surface so that weeds and stubble could be raked up and burned. There was also work to be had digging land drains. A common method in Ambridge was to cut a channel down a field and fill it with thornboughs covered with earth. It took many years before the thorns decayed and compressed too much to carry off excess water. In Penny Hassett horns from the cattle killed at Borchester slaughter-house were used to make continuous primitive drains.

The farm labourer in the last quarter of the nineteenth century lived a hard, bitter life. England was suffering from a deep agricultural depression; cheap wheat from the New World, a series of poor harvests in the seventies and epidemics among livestock drove thousands of small farmers to bankruptcy. They had little charity to spare for the labourers who, like the beasts of burden they tended, were employed for their muscle-power. The labourers worked long hours and often died in harness. If they could no longer work they depended on parish relief and the charity of their children or they went to the Borchester Workhouse.

If he died in Ambridge, the labourer was supplied with an oak coffin lined with cotton wool and a headrest filled with sawdust. Four members of the Sick and Provident Society carried the coffin on their shoulders to church accompanied by two boys with coffin stools, so that the coffin could be set down at intervals for the men to rest.

21

The Archer Photographs

The Archers have been yeoman farmers in Ambridge for generations. The Forrest family, for at least two hundred years, have worked as gamekeepers on the Ambridge estate. Doris Forrest was born in 1900 and married Daniel Archer in 1921, and during her life she collected together photographs not only of the two families, but of Ambridge village life. The photographs, dating mainly from the eighteen sixties to the early nineteen twenties, form a rare and valuable record of rural life as it was.

Benjamin Francis Archer, born 1797, was the tenant farmer at Brookfield until his death in 1864. The photograph must have been taken shortly before he died, because it also shows his grandson, John, aged about six. The Archer family Bible records that John was born in 1858.

Daniel William Archer, grandfather of the present Dan Archer, born 1828, died 1890. He married Elizabeth Simms of Little Croxley, who brought into the marriage £700 and a set of silver spoons. Daniel William spent the money in six months, according to family tradition. The family still possesses three of the spoons.

Taken in Ambridge in about 1890. In the centre is George Forrest, grandfather of Doris Archer and maternal great-grandfather of Philip Archer, the present owner of Brookfield Farm.

Doris, aged about five, helps feed the geese on a neighbour's smallholding.

Thomas Forrest, Doris's uncle, who worked as a carter for an Ambridge hay purveyor. The two horses have the traditional straw 'hats' on their ears to ward off flies during the summer.

Ambridge School annual photograph, 1905. Third from the right, front row, Doris Forrest. Third row, far left, Dan Archer, whom she would marry in 1921.

Lettie Lawson-Hope (holding the whip) pictured outside the Dower House.

Taken by the Ambridge postbox in about 1907, the boy on the far left is John Archer (known as Ben) who married a French Canadian girl, Simone Delamain, and emigrated to Canada.

The milkmaid on the estate farm at Ambridge.

The last squire of Ambridge, Francis Lawson-Hope, seated and holding his shotgun after a morning's rabbit-shooting. Squire Lawson-Hope commanded the 2nd battalion the West Borsetshire Regiment in the First World War, and thirty-five men from the village enlisted under him. He sold the estate in 1954, and Dan Archer bought Brookfield Farm from him.

Dan Archer, aged about six, bottle-feeding lambs at Brookfield in about 1902.

Dan Archer in 1922, leading a team of oxen from Ambridge in the Borchester May Queen celebrations.

The steam locomotive 'Borset' was built for the ill-fated branch line between Borchester and Hollerton Junction, which was completed in 1892 and designed to join Borchester to the Great Western line. The branch line was never profitable and was closed in 1917.

Fat lambs in midsummer at Home Farm, 1900.

Baling hay, 1915. The army had an enormous need for hay for cavalry regiments. The stationary baler was worked by a steam engine, which rammed the hay down (the 'horse's head') and compressed it. The man on the ground facing the camera is holding a 'needle' which was used to separate the bales.

Borchester Carnival, just after the First World War. One of the sailors on the float was John Archer.

The first tractor – in this case a Fordson – brought with it the age of mechanized farming. In this picture Fred Newcombe, estate manager for Squire Lawson-Hope, uses the first tractor to reach Ambridge.

Chipperfield's Circus visited Borchester every summer in the 1920s.

Threshing at Brookfield Farm. The sheaves of corn were pulled from the rick by hand and thrown down into the threshing drum, which was powered by a stationary steam engine. The threshing drum cast out the straw at the back, and the wheat poured out through two funnels at the front. It was always a winter job: the corn was ricked and thatched in the autumn, and waited for the contractor and his two men to come with the steam engine. The farmer had to supply horses to pull the engine to the next farm after threshing was completed.

One of the first potato digging machines. Taken just before the First World War, this picture shows that horses were beginning to take over from oxen in the Ambridge area.

Hare-coursing on Heydon Berrow in the early 1920s.

22

Love and Luck, Marriage and Death

Borsetshire is famous for its rhymes and sayings – although many of them exist, in different forms, in other parts of England. The outstanding beauty of girls from Penny Hassett was always said to be due to their use of wild strawberry leaves as a cosmetic – a secret they were supposed to have guarded jealously from Ambridge girls for hundreds of years. In fact, the 'secret' is revealed in the old English folk-song 'Dabbling in the Dew':

> Pray whither so trippingly, pretty fair maid,
> With your face rosy white and your soft yellow hair?
> Sweet sir, to the well in the summer-wood shade,
> For strawberry leaves make the young maiden fair.

Signs in the sky, pictures in the fire, the scratching of a mouse, the fall of a leaf in a particular way – the country life has always been a matter of omens, portents and charms. Many of those known in Waterley Cross were collected together by the Women's Institute and published in a small booklet in 1948. By talking to the oldest inhabitants of the village, WI members discovered that it was unlucky to cross knives at the table, mend an article of clothing while still wearing it, kill a money spider or spill the salt, pass someone on the stairs, chop down a holly tree or open an umbrella inside the house.

Good luck followed from picking up an umbrella (or pair of gloves), eating grey peas and bacon on Ash Wednesday, or falling downstairs. A wish made when a shooting star was seen always came true – but the person who made the wish always lived to regret it.

Joby Woodford, who works as a woodman on the Ambridge Estate, knows an amazing number of superstitions involving trees, including the belief that is is unlucky to cut elder-blossom without asking permission of the tree itself, and that if a child is beaten with an ash stick he will stop growing. On the other hand, possession of an ash stick is supposed to bring good luck to the owner.

Many of Ambridge's older residents are familiar with 'luck' sayings about animals and birds. If you hear the first cuckoo of the year on your

Doris Archer's mother, Lisa Forrest, photographed in the 1880s. A reputed 'Borsetshire Beauty', she was born Lisa Hart and came from a family of eleven children. Her father was a lawyer's clerk and her marriage to William Forrest was a true love-match – her family thought she had married beneath her station.

left it means bad luck, but on your right hand good luck; if you first see young lambs with their faces towards you it is good, but if you first see their tails it is bad. Mrs Emily Tarbutts, who lived in the village for many years, always said that to hear a robin in the morning meant rain before night, and she was familiar with the belief that to kill a robin would bring the worst luck of all.

Two curious beliefs were remembered by Joe Grundy of Grange Farm: to kill a pig on the wane of the moon means that the bacon will shrink in boiling, but if it is killed at the full, the bacon will swell; and 'if your nose itches you'll be kissed, cursed or vexed by a fool'.

The vision of a 'coming stranger' in the candle or fire is well known, and is listed as an Ambridge saying in Symonds' *Borsetshire Folk-Lore*:

> The coming stranger appears fleetingly in the red-hot patch in the wick of a candle or the thin, flickering leaf which hangs down from the bar of the fire-grate, and tells not only the coming of a stranger but how many strangers and in what humour, before it falls away.

Symonds also relates a curious superstition from Penny Hassett, noted by a visitor from London in 1884:

> A village girl working in the rectory one day said to me: 'Ah! Now you have broken my dream'. On asking what she meant, she replied: 'If anyone dreams of any person or of an event of any kind and someone the next day mentions the name of the person or the circumstances of the dream, then it is broken and you need take no further notice of it, for it will not come true.'

Another remarkable local superstition comes from the *Borchester Echo,* which reported in 1869 that old women had been seen near Waterley Cross (only four miles from Ambridge) catching falling rain on Ascension Day and bottling it for future use – they believed the water would prevent 'heavy bread' if they added a spoonful to the leaven.

The *Borchester Echo*'s 'Curiosity Corner', which ran for several years between the wars, included three rhymes believed to have come from the Ambridge/Penny Hassett area:

A whistling woman and a crowing hen
Are neither good for gods or men

Even-leaved ash, or four-leaved clover,
You'll meet your true love before the day is over.

A gift on the thumb is sure to come;
A gift on the finger is sure to linger.

Unlike many old country cures for illness, which sound illogical but have some basis in fact, many if not most superstitious sayings and rhymes are incomprehensible to the factual, common-sense mind. So, too, is the old Borsetshire horse-test:

One white foot, buy a horse;
Two white feet, try a horse;
Three white feet, look well about him;
Four white feet, go away without him.

Entrance to Brookfield
Farm in autumn.

Marriage has gathered a rich fund of traditions about it (in Borsetshire they used to throw wheat instead of rice for luck) and Martha Woodford, who runs the village shop in Ambridge, vividly remembers the beliefs that surrounded the wedding ceremony during her childhood in Penny Hassett. Today a bride might take the precaution of wearing something borrowed, something blue, etc, and avoid the bridegroom on the morning before the wedding, but the Penny Hassett (and no doubt Ambridge) bride of days gone by had a much more complicated life:

For a start she hadn't to mark her new clothes – her trousseau, you know – with her name before the wedding took place, else it was sure not to happen. Then she had to make sure she didn't get wed in the winter – 'marriage twixt sickle and scythe will never thrive' – and when she went from her home to the church she had to make sure she didn't look back at her old house – that was very unlucky. What was lucky, though, was to meet a grey horse, and I daresay that's why grey horses were used for wedding carriages before the war. When they went into church, once upon a time, the bridesmaid used to carry a cake that the bride had made herself, and make sure the bridegroom ate a bit – that was to keep him faithful. After the ceremony she and her new husband would drink out of a cup with two handles, and when they went to their new home the bride had to have a handful of cinders from her mother's fire and kindle her new fire with them, and she was never supposed to let her fire go out.

After marriage, childbirth, and an even greater confusion of traditions and beliefs. 'A good year for nuts is a good year for babies' was often quoted by Lisa Forrest, who died in 1931, and she told her daughter Doris that when she was a girl a new born child's mouth would immediately be rubbed with 'the treacle of heaven' – a mixture of butter, sugar and honey. It was considered lucky for a child to be born with his face partly covered by the caul – known as the 'mask' – and the mask itself was later valuable, in that its possession was said to safeguard its owner from drowning.

After childbirth it was common practice among cottagers for the new mother to have four days 'holiday' of total seclusion, and during this time she was fed a nourishing food called caundle – a mixture of old ale, oatmeal and sugar. In Ambridge, as elsewhere, it was considered the duty of the squire's wife to provide the caundle and it was the ritual duty of the new father to go to the kitchen door of the hall each day to collect it.

'Caundle wells' are more of a rarity in Borsetshire (though common in Warwickshire) and it was not until this year that the survey team, acting on information found in a scrapbook of early Victorian recollections, found what is thought to be a caundle well in the kitchen of Woodbine Cottage. Measuring twenty-three feet deep and covered by a precariously balanced flagstone, it is an ordinary cottage well that for some reason was selected as the well from which water came for the

A Borsetshire farmyard in 1850.

caundle if the new mother was either teetotal or unable for some reason to drink ale.

Among the possessions of Ambridge church is the nineteenth-century 'christom' made of fine linen edged with lace and presented to the parish as a communal christening gown by Dudley Lawson-Hope in the eighteen twenties. It was meant to be used by families too poor to afford christening gowns for their children and it was the duty of the mother to return it to the vicar when she returned to be 'churched'.

Common Borsetshire beliefs associated with childbirth were listed by Symonds, and they show a not unreasonable dependence on charms and luck-rituals in an age when infant mortality was horrifyingly high.

> It is thought unlucky for a child to go down before he goes up, and if born in a bedroom upstairs he will be lifted on a chair before being allowed down the stairs. It is unlucky for him to see himself in a pool or a mirror immediately after birth, and it is unlucky to weigh a baby or cut his nails before twelve months (else he will grow up light-fingered). A red ribbon round a baby's neck is commonly thought to prevent convulsions, and infants are still commonly rubbed all over with snow, if snow lies on the ground on the day of their birth.

Infant remedies were both strange and terrible: roasted mouse was thought to cure whooping cough and stop bed-wetting, brains of hare were thought good for ailing children, and in Waterley Cross it was firmly believed that the cure for 'white mouth' was to give the child a young yellow frog to suck.

Death and its portents have always gripped the human imagination.

The cry of the screech-owl, pigeons flying against the window, accidental coffin-shaped creases in a table cloth, the curling tallow of a candle, a toad crossing a path – all these have been commonly regarded as signs of approaching death. Borsetshire sayings on the subject include:

> If in your house a man shoulders a spade,
> For you or your kinsfolk a grave is made.
>
> Buy a broom in May
> You're sure to sweep a corpse away.
>
> If your bees fall sick and die
> One of your house is sure to die.

There is an old Ambridge tradition that if a grave is left open on a Sunday there will be another death before the month is out, and another that the transplanting of parsley means a death in the family owning the garden within a year. Walter Gabriel tells the story of a man from Hollerton who accidentally cut through a root of white bryony (known locally as mandrake) while digging the footings for the Ambridge primary school in 1909, and was so frightened that he could no longer work. A few days later he fell down some steps and broke his neck. (A similar incident occurred near Stratford-on-Avon at about the same time.) Walter Gabriel also recalls his grandmother's knowledge of death-rituals:

> They mostly sound daft, but folk were very superstitious then, you see – ordinary folk, though I daresay the vicar's wife was just as bad, she never would let snowdrops into the church. Anyway, when somebody died in a house there were any number of things you had to do and check up on. For a start, every door lock had to be undone, then the bees had to be told – a chap had to knock on each hive with a key and tell them the master was dead, otherwise they'd have all buzzed off. In the house you had to make sure you didn't look in a mirror in the same room as the corpse was lying, or you'd see the reflection of the dead person in it. Then, if the hands of the corpse stayed clammy and wet, it meant another death was on the way. Black horses were always used to pull the hearse to the church, and if one of those black horses turned its head towards a cottage door and neighed, well, there'd be a death in that house within the twelvemonth. Another thing was the corpse way. It's still there, in Ambridge, going from Grundy's farm down to the church. They called it the corpse way because if a corpse is carried over private land it becomes a public footpath for ever afterwards, and I believe that's as true now as it ever was.

Corpse ways, or church ways, are not singular to the Ambridge area. There is one between Stratford-on-Avon and Wilmcote and another between Whitchurch and Binton in Warwickshire.

One custom, common in Borsetshire as elsewhere, has not died out: the church bells, preceding a funeral. Three strokes for a child, six for a woman, and nine for a man, followed by one stroke for each year of the dead person's life.

23

Ghosts, Witches and Demons

The folk-lore of Borsetshire is rich in tales of ghosts, goblins, witches and demons. In Ambridge alone, Walter Gabriel knows of six places that are said to be haunted and can recount at length the tragic stories that belong to each.

The most famous Borsetshire ghost is, of course, the Wandering White Lady of Loxley Barratt, but her history is too well known to be recorded here. The most feared apparition is undoubtedly the Hob Hound, who was described in a letter to the *Borsetshire Gentleman's Magazine* in 1844:

> The working people of the three villages, Hollerton, Penny Hassett and Ambridge, have a pitiable belief in this creature, the appearance of which is said by them to have been responsible for the death of a poor woman on the turnpike on Wednesday last, whose face was found to be savagely twisted when her body was discovered. We might well wonder whether it was the sight of the Hob Hound, with its red glowing eyes and poisonous breath, or the effects of hunger and cold that caused the dead woman's agony, but in Ambridge the people will have it that the Hob Hound was running that night, on his accustomed course, with a wild horseman galloping at breakneck speed behind him and urging him to run ever faster towards his prey. Furthermore, when the wind is high the people listen for the huntsman's horn, bolt their doors and say that the devil is coming to collect his own. Only the traveller who rides a horse shod with iron shoes is believed by them to be safe.

Walter Gabriel claims that Arthur Conan Doyle used the story of the Hob Hound as a basis for *The Hound of the Baskervilles* but there is no other evidence to support the possibility. It is possible, however, that Edgar Allan Poe was inspired to write *The Fall of the House of Usher* by the story of Charity Box, who died of the plague in 1568 and was interred in the family vault in Borbury church. A fortnight later another member of the family died and the vault was reopened. Charity's body was found upright, leaning against the wall. She had been buried while still alive and in her torment had bitten halfway through her arm. Her ghost now haunts the path between the church and Borbury Manor.

The only other literary association claimed for Borsetshire ghosts is the tradition that Shakespeare based Ophelia on Ann Timmins, a girl from Edgeley who drowned herself in the Am in 1553 after searching in vain for a serving man who had been dismissed by her father after he asked for her hand in marriage. She was seventeen and her ghost haunts the Am below Long Meadow.

The Bull has an upstairs room in which ghostly tapping noises were heard as recently as January 1981. Sid Perks, the landlord, can offer no logical explanation.

We thought at first it was the television cable that was loose and banging against the outside wall, but after I'd fixed it the noise was still there. I spent a lot of time and trouble before Christmas repainting and redecorating the room, and fitting a little desk under the window – making a sort of study for our Lucy. She 's a bright kid, but a public house is full of noise and distractions and I've thought for a long time she needs somewhere quiet to do her reading. She won't use that room though. Not by herself. She'd sooner sit downstairs at the kitchen table, even with the noise from the Ploughman's banging against her ears and Polly going past her every five minutes getting ice from the fridge and peanuts from the store room and what have you. Nobody really knows what the tapping's supposed to be. There was some talk about a soldier being trapped behind a blocked up doorway but I can't credit that – not unless his ghost is suspended in thin air just on top of our inn sign, because the blocked up doorway is in an outside wall. John Tregorran told us about this drummer boy who died here and the noise does sound a bit like a drum. Four of us heard it one afternoon. Me, Polly, Pat Archer and Shula.

Black Dogs loom large in the folk-lore of Borsetshire and are said to manifest themselves in a dozen or so places including Ambridge, Waterley Cross, Borbury and Edgeley. In his *Recollections of an old Borsetshire Clergyman* published in 1905, the Reverend Lionel Thompson wrote about the Ambridge dog:

'The sexton assured me that the dog had been seen a dozen times within the past ten years, and had first appeared after an unfortunate incident in which the lid came loose on a coffin which was being taken from Back Lane to the church. The sexton himself banged the lid down again with a stone, but believes a nail must have pierced the skull inside, allowing the spirit to escape.

The only modern phenomenon in Ambridge seems to have been a dim blue light which was seen to hover over a group of gravestones in St Stephen's churchyard in the autumn of 1933. Tom Forrest can remember the stir it caused. 'When one old boy said he'd seen this blue light buzzing about the gravestones everyone blamed it on bad beer, but then other folk reckoned to have seen it, till one night it was reported moving through the trees of the deer park, heading up over Blossom Hill. It was never seen again.'

The best documented Ambridge ghost is undoubtedly that of Squire Lawson – 'Mad Lawson' or 'Black Lawson' as he is called in different tales – who appears on Heydon Berrow at midnight on Lady Day (25 March). The ghost is believed to be that of John Lawson, who was born in 1669 and grew up in genteel poverty as the family struggled to pay off the debts contracted during the Civil War period. In 1689, when he was twenty, John was married to Annabel Hope, whose dowry was intended to restore the family fortunes. It was a disastrous move. Embittered by the penury of his youth and forced into marriage with a merchant's daughter ten years his senior, John Lawson quickly went to the bad and acquired a reputation through half the county for hard-drinking, gambling and reckless behaviour. Few writers in the past have concerned themselves with the sorry plight of Annabel, who was uprooted from her affectionate family and journeyed one late September day along the track from the village to the old, decaying manor house of Lyttleton (now Home Farm), surrounded by the dense woodland of Leader's Wood and the Forest of Am, where she had to live among a family that was cold, resentful and caring only for her money. Two of Annabel's letters home to her sister Betty survive in the Hope Collection and they show a woman of intelligence and good humour, only gradually beaten down by the circumstances of her life. The first letter was written in August 1690 and also offers a revealing – if romantic – insight into Ambridge village conditions:

> You wish to know how I pass my time here. I rise early in the morning and go round the house till I am weary of that, and into the garden until it grows too hot. About ten o'clock I think of making me ready, and when that's done go into my husband's chamber, and from there to dinner, where we sit in silent state in a room that would hold many more. The heat of the day I spend reading, then about six or seven o'clock walk out along the river to the common lands where many young wenches keep sheep and cows and sit under the trees singing ballads. There is some vast difference in their voices to the old shepherdesses I have read of, but, trust me, I think these are as innocent as those. I talk to them, and find they want nothing to make them the happiest people in the world but the knowledge that they are so. Often, during our discourse, one looks about her and spies her cows going into the corn, and of a sudden away they all run, and I that am not so nimble stay behind and watch them drive home their cattle, until it is time for me to retire too. When I have supped, I go into the garden, where I sit and wish you all were with me.

Hay-harvest in the nineteenth century.

After a year in Ambridge she was clearly ignored and lonely, dining with her husband 'in silent state' and left to her own devices for the rest of the day. The second letter to survive shows a mood of deep depression.

All that I can say, then, is that I resolve on nothing but to arm myself with patience, to resist nothing that is laid upon me, nor struggle for what I have no hope to get. I have nothing more to do with the world, but to expect when I shall be so happy as to leave it.

But it was John Lawson, not Annabel, who was soon to leave the world. He had already dismissed his bailiff and on Lady Day 1697, after spending the evening collecting rents from his tenant farmers, and no doubt drinking their cider, he was thrown from his horse and broke his neck. This, at least, is the account passed down through the Lawson-Hope family and told to Doris Archer by Lettie Lawson-Hope in the nineteen fifties. Symonds' *Borchester Folk-Lore,* however, has another version of events:

Folly and bad language, hard-drinking and hard-riding, finally caught up with Black Lawson. He rode to hounds every day and swore constantly, showing contempt for the devil himself. One night, returning from the hunt, two stray hounds startled his mount. Swearing terrible blasphemies, Black Lawson galloped his terrified horse across Heydon Berrow until it fell, breaking both its own neck and the neck of its rider. Since then Black Lawson has several times been seen at midnight on Lady Day, riding his mount across the common, accompanied by two hell hounds who follow him till dawn.

Other traditions surrounding Black Lawson include the belief that on his mad rides he calls on travellers to open gates for him – and his command must on no account be obeyed, or the person will be carried off and made a member of the baleful Wild Hunt which rides the high ground from Hassett to Lakey Hill.

In Borsetshire the devil himself has been known from early Elizabethan times as 'the naughty man', and cow parsley, for some long-forgotten reason, is widely known as naughty man's parsley. Place names frequently have association with the devil – there is a Hob Acre at Bridge Farm, Ambridge, a Hob's Meadow at Valley Farm and a Hob's Lane at Edgeley.

After ghosts and devils, Borsetshire folk have always been fascinated by fairies and hobgoblins, which can be either kind or wicked. Cobs and knops are the most terrible, together with Old Grim, who 'do like a skritch owl cry at sicke men's windows'. The flibbertigibbet is a pathetic demon who wails and snuffles from dusk to dawn (as a Borsetshire countryman would say, 'From daygate to cock-crow,') and will o'the wisps are mischievous spirits who shine lights to lead men astray in darkness. Someone who has been misled by a will o'the wisp is said to be 'mabled'.

The friendliest spirit is a dobbie, a creature peculiar to Borsetshire and Warwickshire, who lives in farmhouses and is exceptionally lazy. Dobbies inhabit the same house for generations of human occupation, watching over the family, doing a bit of dusting or sweeping up and supposedly protecting the hens from foxes. Curiously enough, although several farmers in Ambridge knew of dobbies and joked about having one, the only farm where there is any former reference to a dobbie is Grange Farm – and neither Joe nor Eddie Grundy even knew what a dobbie was. The reference comes again from the invaluable *Borsetshire Recollected,* which was published in 1911:

> The dobbie must feel the malign influence of these sceptical times more than most, and must rue the coming of an age in which man believes only in science and the money in his pocket, and thinks nothing exists that he cannot see by electric light. Borsetshire's old familiar spirits, that have inhabited the far Western glades and verdant pastures of the old forest of Arden since long before Will Shakespeare, must complain bitterly at their midnight revelries; Queen Mab and Tib, and Puck, and the poor will o'the wisps whose lamps now seem so dim next to the lamps of the motor car! But none have suffered like the dobbies, living in their remote farmhouses amid families who no longer believe in their existence! How can they be freed to enter the fairy kingdom, when humans of the twentieth century know not how to free them? On what do they live, now the custom of leaving milk and manchet has gone? Only in Ambridge, at Grange Farm, is a dobbie still known to thrive in the affection of a human family, and still, according to the farmer, sweeps the kitchen of a night and eats his bread.

Grange Farm, which is still believed to be inhabited by a friendly dobbie.

Manchet (the medieval Lord's Bread) was a wheaten roll of high quality and traditionally given only to dobbies who were held in high regard. There cannot have been many of these, as dobbies have always been noted for their extreme indolence, reluctance to guard the farm buildings on cold winter's nights, and habit of sweeping dust under the carpets. Only when the family they guard is in extreme trouble are they known to exert themselves. On these occasions, however, the family can reward their dobbie by granting it freedom: the daughter of the house must sew a suit of scarlet material and leave it at night in the farm kitchen, together with a bowl of milk and some bread. If in the morning the bread and milk are still there, but the scarlet suit is gone, then the farm dobbie has escaped to the freedom of fairyland.

In Borsetshire ghosts and hobgoblins abound, but there are relatively few tales involving witchcraft and the dabbling by humans in the supernatural. This is probably because of the county's geographical location: witchcraft was always a more feared and powerful presence in Scotland and the eastern part of England where religious puritanism was strong. In the more easy-going and tolerant west, witches were believed in but rarely persecuted. Nevertheless, symbols of protection against witchcraft can be seen carved over the doors of many old cottages, laurels were planted to keep witches away and it was well known even twenty years ago that rowan leaves ties to the head of a bed would ward off evil. In Penny Hassett in 1734 invisible witches were smoked out of a room in the parsonage by the use of hemlock, sloe, rue and rosemary leaves, which were burnt by men blessed beforehand in the church.

A strange test for witchcraft was practised by Borchester schoolchildren in the late nineteenth century, when girls were made to whirl round and round holding a snail at arm's length, while other children stood in a circle and chanted:

> Snail, snail, come out of your shell
> Or we'll kill your mother and father.

If the snail did emerge, then the girl holding the shell was called a witch.

In Ambridge, Walter Gabriel has vivid memories of an old woman, reputed to be a witch, who lived in a cottage next to the smallholding he farmed before the Second World War:

She was called Mother Horsefall, and she lived at Toad Cottage, down Back Lane. It wasn't really called Toad Cottage, but that's what the youngsters

called it, and even though a solicitor chap bought it in about nineteen thirty-eight and changed its name to April Cottage, it was still Toad Cottage to me and a good few others. Anyway, Mother Horsefall lived there and everybody said she could draw an invisible line across Back Lane and no animal would ever go over it. In those days a grocer from Penny Hassett used to come round once a fortnight with his horse-drawn van, and sure enough his horse would always stop outside Toad Cottage and wouldn't budge for anything. She'd drawn her line, you see, and while the grocer – Gilbert he was called – while he was ranting and raving at his horse, Mother Horsefall would be pinching things from his van – soap, tea, whatever it was she wanted. She was invisible, of course – or else she'd turn herself into a rabbit, but I don't see how a rabbit could carry much in the way of groceries. Gilbert got himself a motor-van in the end.

Another thing they said about Mother Horsefall. One day a bloke caught a rabbit and got the surprise of his life when it bit his finger. He was so enraged he gave it a thump round the head, and while he was doing that it kicked out and somehow got away from him. Well, next day there was Mother Horsefall limping about with a great bruise over her eye and the side of her head.

When she died they found a witch's ladder in her cottage – that's a rope with a loop in the end, and thorns and feathers stuck along it at intervals. She could get into anywhere with that ladder.

Penny Hassett seems to have suffered more than its share of witches in the eighteenth century. Apart from the invisible witches in the parsonage, there was Mother Deane, who buried three husbands and cast fatal spells on most of her neighbours' cattle before dying herself in 1742. According to the story still told (with much gusto) in the Griffin's Head at Penny Hassett, the people of the village were delighted when Mother Deane died, and buried her in an iron coffin. When they returned past her cottage, however, they heard her singing and when they looked inside they found her frying bacon and eggs. The vicar of Edgeley was called in (he had a reputation for dealing with witches, or 'wise women' as they were known) and he exorcised her, turning her first into a greyhound and then sending her racing across the countryside until she fell, exhausted, into a farm pond (between the present Bridge Farm and Home Farm, Ambridge) which is still known as Witch's Pond. Through some sort of dispensation, Mother Deane can return to her cottage in Penny Hassett at the rate of one cock stride a year, and the locals have computed that she will not materialize for another 1800 years.

An even sadder fate befell a wedding party at Netherbourne in the sixteenth century. The Netherbourne Stones are well known Megalithic monuments, the finest in East Borsetshire, that belong to the Beaker Period of around 2000 BC. Jack Woolley is friendly with Lord and Lady Netherbourne, however, and over dinner in his private rooms at Grey Gables one night they told him quite a different story of their provenance:

The Netherbourne Stones.

The history of the Netherbourne Stones is one of the most fascinating tales I've ever heard – and I don't think it was because we were sitting by candlelight in my oak-panelled dining room when Lady Netherbourne recounted it, although atmosphere is very important when it comes to stories of the supernatural. Anyway, according to the story a young Netherbourne couple got married on a Saturday – this was in the sixteenth or seventeenth century, a good few years ago – and they held their reception in a field. They invited their friends along, provided a few jars of cider or mead I expect, and hired a fiddler to play some music. It was a pretty wild affair by all accounts, and the bride was a beautiful, wanton sort of creature who danced madly all night long. At midnight, though, the fiddler refused to play anymore because it was now Sunday.

The wanton bride – Lady Netherbourne's words – ordered him to play on and cursed him, but he still refused and packed his fiddle away and went off into the darkness. At that moment another fiddler appeared and said he was willing to play on. The wanton bride was delighted, and so was everybody else. First the new fiddler played a slow tune, but the wanton bride yelled at him to play faster, as she whirled round the fire with her hair flowing behind her. So the fiddler played a faster tune, one that nobody could resist. They all danced as fast as they could, and suddenly they found they couldn't stop dancing, even though they cried out to the fiddler to stop. The faster he played the faster they danced, all night long, until at cock-crow the fiddler suddenly stopped, and as the sun came up the dancers were all seen to have been turned to stone.

The grim fiddler conforms very much to the medieval view of the wizard; a man with great powers, cold even in his kindness, cruel when he wrought vengeance on those who for some reason had offended him or lost the protection of the church.

There was only one charm effective against wizards according to *Borsetshire Folk-Lore*, and that was a square of parchment with five words written on it, each appearing four times when read backwards and from bottom to top:

S	A	T	O	R
A	R	E	P	O
T	E	N	E	T
O	P	E	R	A
R	O	T	A	S

The charm actually goes back to Roman times and has been found inscribed on a third century drinking mug at Cirencester.

Through the centuries the functions of witches and wizards changed. They became wise women and cunning men, concerned not with the fate of nations and the weaving of spells, but more commonly with the treatment of warts and ringworm. Simon Cooper at Ambridge recalled an incident from when he was a boy:

My mother used to go feeding the calves every day with great buckets of milk, and they'd push and shove so it got spilt all over the place. Then the calves got ringworm, and before you knew it my Mum had ringworm – you could see them all up her arms. Then she passed it to me and I had ringworms up my arms. We went to the doctor but it didn't do any good, so in the end we went to see an old woman in the village and she had some bits of sheet torn up, and she sort of passed them through the pages of a Bible and muttered some sort of spell, then wrapped the bandages round our arms. Two days later we were all cleared up.

A 'cunning man' lived at Edgeley until 1935 when he disappeared without trace. He was said to be able to cure warts by placing a penknife lightly on top of them, then cutting a strip of bark from an elm tree. He assured his patients that as the bark withered, so would the warts. In Ambridge it was believed warts could be cured by rubbing a penny on them, then burying it in the garden. Piles could be cured if the person afflicted carried a conker round with him for two weeks. Toothache (which was believed to be caused by a tiny white worm in the gum) was treated with cloves.

Martha Woodford remembers several other common country remedies from her childhood in Penny Hassett.

If a child had something wrong with his eyes – not serious, but swelling and redness – then he was treated with the juice of the greater celandine. They used to say swallows took it back to the nest for their young when they were born blind. Meadowsweet was good for pains and cold in the stomach, and you could help a cough by passing through a flock of sheep. The best thing for a cold was always goose fat rubbed on the chest. Cure anything that would. Nobody likes lying all sticky and stinking of goose fat.

There are several cases recorded in the *Borchester Echo* of children being treated for hernia in the nineteenth century by passing them through the split trunk of an ash sapling grown from seed.

24

The Village Craftsman

Today Ambridge has a village shop (selling mainly food, tobacco and newspapers), a pub and a garage, as well as St Stephen's Church and the village hall. A mile outside the village, Grey Gables Country Club includes a garden centre, country park and small golf course. Since the retirement of Dr McLaren five years ago the nearest doctor lives at Penny Hassett. The vet and travelling farrier come to the village, on request, from Borchester. The bus service was withdrawn in the sixties and the village school closed at the same time. There are 97 houses (including Manorfield Close Old Folks' Bungalows) and 381 inhabitants.

In 1850 the *History, Gazetteer and Directory of Borsetshire* listed Ambridge as:

A parish and pleasant village five miles south of Borchester. It contains 2,210 acres of land. In 1841 here were 79 houses with 394 inhabitants. The rateable value was £2259. In 1803 the parish rates were £441.11.2d at 6s.6d in the pound. The abbot of St Mary's, Worcester, was an early possessor of the lordship, which now resides with the Lawson-Hope family. A carrier calls on Thursday from Hollerton to Borchester, and returns.
Directory
Blower T. Baker and miller
Box R. Shoemaker
Clarke T. Shopkeeper
Hands R. Hurdle-maker
Morris J. Schoolmaster
Mumford R. Carpenter
Perrin S. Publican and maltster
Rev. Richard Leadbeater Vicar
Slatter J. Carpenter
Gabriel J. Blacksmith
Waters C. Farrier
Rouse J. Wheelwright

The village in 1850 milled the corn grown in its own fields, baked its own bread and brewed its own ale. It made its own furniture and tools, its carts, field-gates, coffins and cribs, its boots and smocks. Children

The village roadmender, 1890.

were taught at the village school and the village church. The shop sold food the cottagers could not make or grow themselves: salt, pepper and tea, and large quantities of cheese and treacle, as well as working clothes and patent medicines. (The account books of Waterley Cross village shop 1864–78 are available at Borchester Museum.) Although not listed in the 1850 directory, there was an Ambridge man who made his living from building field ponds. Of the 394 inhabitants, everyone except the squire, vicar and schoolmaster must have lived on the land or by one of

John Gabriel, the Ambridge blacksmith, photographed in 1892, four years before the birth of his grandson, Walter Gabriel, who still lives in the village. His great grandson, Nelson Gabriel, is a Borchester businessman.

the trades associated with it – blacksmith, wheelwright, farrier, hurdle-maker, bootmaker and carpenter.

The village was a busy place. In the early 1960s an old resident could remember how, before the turn of the century, the Bull used to open at six o'clock in the morning to cater for the hay wagons on their way into Borchester. 'That was before Dora (*Defence of the Realm Act*) brought in the licensing laws, of course.' Several of the older inhabitants today can remember stopping on the way to school to watch the huge lathe-wheel spinning in the wheelwright's shop, or help throw an ox to the ground outside the smithy, so that it could be re-shod. The village craftsmen started at six o'clock in the morning and worked a twelve-hour day.

Chief among the village craftsmen was the blacksmith – at least, so the blacksmiths always claimed. In King Alfred's day, according to tradition, the King honoured his tailor higher than his smith at a banquet and the smith refused to work any longer. As a result the mason and carpenter could not get tools, horses could not be shod and weapons could not be sharpened. King Alfred then raised the blacksmith to first place and the tailor in revenge snipped the bottom of the smith's leather apron with his scissors. To this day blacksmiths' aprons have a traditional fringe, to remind them of the tailor's perfidious action and to help sweep away metal shavings as they work.

The blacksmiths' pride was maintained by the Ambridge smiths, John and Nelson Gabriel. Over the door of their smithy (the site is now occupied by the garage) was the motto: 'By hammer and hand, all arts do stand.' The smith made the scythes and tools for the farms, hinges for field gates and cottage doors, metal parts for farm wagons, locks and candle-holders, fire-irons and plough-shares. John Gabriel charged a penny to mend a child's broken play hoop – a tricky repair, as the weld often overheated, melting away the hoop itself.

The blacksmith worked closely with the wheelwright when it came to fitting metal tyres to the wooden wheels of farm wagons. First the perimeter of the wooden wheel was measured with a traveller, then a flat iron bar was formed into a circle on a tyre bender and welded into a hoop fractionally smaller than the wooden wheel. The hoop was then heated to make it expand, and hammered onto the wheel while it was red-hot. Water was quickly poured over it and as the tyre shrank the woodwork joints were forced tighter together.

The Ambridge blacksmith was also the village farrier. (A farrier pure and simple was listed in the 1850 directory, but does not seem to have prospered. The 1880 directory listed only N. Gabriel as farrier and blacksmith.) In Ambridge the job of shoeing animals was an exhausting business because oxen continued to be used in the Borsetshire hill country for years after other parts of the Midlands had gone over to the horse. The ox had advantages to the farmer: it was cheaper to feed, needing bulk rather than quality; its hooves did not pad down ploughed ground in the wet; it did not require a dry, windproof stable; and at the end of its days it could be sold as meat. The disadvantage to the farrier was that an ox could never be taught to lift up its hooves and always had to be shod lying down. Several people were needed to 'throw' the animal and sit on its neck while new shoes were fitted.

The village carpenter was among the busiest of men, but had a reputation for being more peaceable and sympathetic than the smith, partly because the nature of his work was the shaping of wood rather than the hammering of iron and partly because the carpenter also doubled as the village undertaker. The Mumfords for the 1850 directory were a famous family, running the carpentry and undertaking business for more than half a century. 'A job for Mumford' meant that someone had died, and Mumford or his son would soon be measuring the corpse with their length of black rope, knotting it once for the length and again for the width. Mumford was renowned for selecting coffin-wood with beautiful grain-markings and for his skill at curving the coffin sides, by sawing the grain partially on the inside and softening the outer grain with boiling water. Few village coffin-makers could manage anything better then the usual straight-sided box.

The carpenter in the nineteenth century selected his wood when it was still standing, and after the trees were felled and trimmed they were taken to his yard to await the arrival of the travelling sawyers. The sawing of timber into planks and posts was a skilled craft: the top-sawyer stood on top of the tree trunk itself while the bottom-sawyer stood below in the saw-pit, and they used an eight-foot-long two-man saw to cut through the wood. It was a skill that vanished, with little regret, when steam-driven saws were introduced, for it was hard, back-breaking work.

Once cut, the wood was stacked until it was seasoned – which could take up to ten years in the case of elm. Every wood had its own uses. Elm was used for floor and coffin boards, and for the shafts of wagons and carts. Beech made yokes for water carriers and milkmaids, and beer funnels. Ash was a general purpose wood, used frequently for wheelbarrows, handcarts and tool handles. Sycamore was the 'fancy' wood, popular for kitchen table-tops because of its creamy whiteness, and for bowls, skimmers, churns, spoons, butter prints and cheese moulds. Wych elm was saved for thrashing floors because of its hardness and smoothness. Oak was for furniture, beams, field gates and cow stalls. Cleft heart of oak was used for wheel spokes.

The Mumfords made oak furniture that can still be found in Ambridge cottages today (oak benches ordered by the Parochial Church Council for use in the village school in 1856 were recently found in the former Field Studies Centre at Nightingale Farm) and a Mumford wheelbarrow is on display at Churcham Farm Museum. But they did not make the massive farm wagons or wheels that were needed in every rural community, because that was the job of Rouse the wainwright.

The Ambridge wainwright's shop with its thatched roof stood at the point where Back Lane joins the main village street, and from it for many hours of the day could be heard the hum of the great hand-turned wheel that worked the lathe for turning naves. The wainwright became commonly known as the wheelwright during the nineteenth century because wheels made up the most skilled part of his work. It was a great event when a new wain – or farm wagon – was ordered. Months of work were involved building the wagon of timber and iron, with its

Thomas Rouse, the Ambridge wheelwright, outside his 'shop' in 1889.

traditional bright yellow body and venetian red undercarriage, its rave bands picked out in black. A wagon had to be light but strong, every vital fibre of wood had to be left, every unnecessary part shaved away. The making of a farm wagon was not profitable, but it earned the goodwill of the farmer, and every four years the wagon came back to be repainted.

The humblest of the village craftsmen was the bootmaker, who worked in the downstairs room of his cottage for long hours and was generally as close to poverty as the labourers who were his customers. The boots were made from tough, bark-tanned leather and the soles were hand-stitched, each hole pierced with an awl before the waxed thread was passed through and pulled tight. Boots had to be strong and waterproof, for the farm labourer depended on them more than on any other article of clothing and few men could afford more than one new pair of boots a year. Bootmaking was a trade traditionally reserved for the village cripple or a child too weak to work in the fields. A good bootmaker, nevertheless, was probably more important to the well-being of the village than any of its other craftsmen. He knew every foot in the village, every corn and misshapen toe, and he custom-built his boots accordingly. A bad bootmaker made his customers suffer from his carelessness every day of the year.

Perhaps the saddest decline of a rural craft is that of the woodlander. The occupations of hurdle-maker and wattle-maker were old at the time of the Norman Conquest and were still flourishing in Ambridge a century ago. They can never return because ploughing subsidies have caused the widespread grubbing out of wooded hillsides during the past fifty years. The hurdle-maker did more than construct the wooden hurdles needed on every farm: he was the man who leased a spinny by the year and took from it wood for himself and for the carpenter, who made ladders and hay racks, selling what remained to the men who made up the bundles of faggots used to light bake-ovens. The hurdle-maker knew how to harvest the living woodland, cutting out willow, beech and sycamore as he required it, and ash and hazel from stools every ten years. The wood itself benefited from his activities.

The old crafts have gone and the new crafts that have replaced them are less obviously a part of the rural scene. The Ambridge carpenter now works for a Borchester building firm, the plumber and electrician work in Hollerton. Farm workers themselves are rated as craftsmen – they know how to inject pigs against iron deficiency and service a tractor, but few now have the skill to lay a hedge correctly.

The early morning sounds of the wainwright's wheel and the blacksmith's hammer have been replaced by the sound of cars and vans carrying today's craftsmen to their occupations elsewhere.

25

The Country Wife

The famous *Churcham Book of Husbandry* lists the duties of the Borsetshire housewife in Tudor times:

Make malte, washe and wrynge, and make hay, shere corne, in time of neede help to fyll the muck wayne, dryve the plough, loode haye, corne, and suche other, ride to market to sel hither butter, chese, mylke, egges, chekens, capons, hennes, pygges, gese and all manner of corne.

By the mid-nineteenth century only the most unfortunate and ill-used of wives were required to fill the muck cart and do the ploughing, but otherwise very little had changed. The womenfolk were expected to milk the cows and make the butter, tend the calves and the hens and go to market, brew the beer, cook the food, bear the children and turn

Doris Archer milking one of the four cows kept at Brookfield Farm in 1922, a year after her marriage to Dan Archer.

out into the fields for haymaking and corn harvest. A Borchester rhyme of 1820 indicates that the urban housewife fared slightly better.

> Rock the cradle, tend the table,
> Blow the fire and spin,
> Take your cup and drink it up,
> Then call your neighbours in.

A more romantic picture is drawn by an unknown eighteenth century writer quoted in *Borsetshire Recalled*. The country wife, he said, renewed the springs of life by her flawless faith and love and purity.

> All her excellences stand in her so silently, as if they had stolen upon her without her knowledge. She doth not, with lying long in bed, spoil both her complexion and conditions: nature hath taught her too, immoderate sleep is rust to the soul . . . The golden ears of corn fall and kiss her feet when she reaps them, as if they wished to be bound and led prisoner by the same hand that felled them. Her breath is her own; which scents all the year long of June, like a new-made hay-cock. She makes her hand hard with labour, and her heart soft with pity.

The Ambridge farmer's wife would have agreed, at least, that her hands were hard with labour and that she had little time to sleep. The days of the week were filled with duties that could not be neglected. If she failed to make butter, the family economy would collapse; if she failed to make bread, the family would starve.

Baking day in Ambridge was a Friday, when the domed, brick-lined ovens in every substantial farmhouse and cottage were in full use. To heat the oven, bundles of dry brushwood were lit and kept burning for two hours until the base of the oven was covered evenly with hot ash. While this was happening the dough was rising in front of the open fire, marked with a cross to prevent the devil from sitting on it. When the oven was hot the ashes were quickly raked out and the bricks mopped with a damp cloth. The loaves were placed at the back of the oven and cakes next to the door, which was blocked with a massive piece of oak called the ditless and sealed with wet rags. Borsetshire people still use the phrase 'in with the bread and out with the cakes' to describe someone who rushes into a venture and then quickly abandons it.

In damp weather, when bread went mouldy before the end of the week, cottagers used to eat a 'boiled bread dinner' – stale bread cooked over the fire with a little butter or salt. Another common meal in times of poverty was hog's pudding, made by stuffing chitlings with a type of coarse oatmeal used for pig food called cutlings. The mill at Loxley Barratt is still called Cutling Mill and up until the early years of this century there was a stall selling nothing but cutlings at Borchester Market. The owner and his wife used to go from village to village during the week with a pony which had two sacks slung over its back, one containing cutlings and the other fine quality oatmeal.

To make hog's pudding, the cottager's wife boiled the cutlings in

Brookfield Farm.

milk mixed with fat (if she was lucky enough to have any) and a little pennyroyal. After this the mixture was stuffed into the chitlings, which were then cooked. The puddings were inclined to burst, and the traditional way to prevent this was to hang one of the parson's old wigs in the chimney. Those unable to procure a parson's wig had to content themselves with pricking the chitlings with a needle.

Milking the cows and making butter were the main jobs for women on the nineteenth-century farm. On small farms the cows were milked in the field during summer. The farmer's wife or daughter would go out with two pails suspended from a yoke slung across her shoulders and carrying her small, three-legged milking stool. The milk would be left to stand in a vat for twelve hours and then be skimmed and strained through a sye bowl, a circular wooden dish with a bottom of fine gauze. Once a week the cream would be made into butter (this, indeed, was the purpose of keeping cows; the actual milk was either consumed by the family or fed back to the calves). To make butter, the cream was salted, then placed in a churn and stirred. It was weary work and the farm women used to sing:

> Churn, butter churn,
> Come, butter, come,
> The great bull of Felpersham
> Shan't have none.

The churn stood on the floor, the churn pole moved up and down, and the women's backs ached, but sometimes, for no accountable reason, the butter refused to come. A silver spoon was then thrown into the cream as a charm against witchcraft (witches' spells being powerless against sterling silver) and if this failed and the witch herself was believed to have passed into the churn, a red-hot poker was thrust in to disturb her milky repose.

Cheese was made on Ambridge's two biggest farms, Home Farm and Bull Farm (*Borsetshire Gazetteer*, 1872) and the two farms joined together to send a wagon to the great September Cheese Fair at Darrington. The wagon had on it a guardian spirit in the shape of a small cheese made to represent a hare. The cheese itself was the old Borsetshire Blue, which was actually rippled with green because of the thin layers of chopped sage added before it was put into the huge farm cheese press.

From the first milk of a newly-calved cow came the rich fluid known generally as beestings but always called cherry curds in Borsetshire and South Warwickshire. Mixed with raisins and flavoured with cinnamon, the milk is still a favourite in the Ambridge area, either eaten like yoghurt or baked in the oven, where it sets quickly into a thick natural pudding.

Farms did their own brewing, and it was traditionally women's work. There were two ale-making times, March and October. In March an infusion of ale hoof (*Nepeta glechona*) and nettle shoots was

The Ambridge Sunday School Outing, 1910.

sometimes added and after the brewing neighbours were called in to 'take the first shot' by dipping crusts of bread into the new beer.

The farmer's wife made her beer from malt (rarely using hops) and also brewed beer from coltsfoot, mangels and parsnips. Two strong beers popular in Ambridge had their own names, according to Walter Gabriel – 'plum gerkum' and 'rhubarb whappy'.

Ale-making in Borchester and at country ale-houses was strictly regulated by the local magistrates and is one area of local history that is fully documented. As far back as 1405 ale brewed for the Feast of the Holy Cross was authorized to be sold at 1½d a gallon for 'gude beere', 1d a gallon for 'peneyale' and ½d a gallon for 'smallale'.

At the Cat and Fiddle on the Ambridge to Borchester road an eighteenth-century rhyme painted on wood hangs behind the bar and tells the names – by strength – of local beers:

Black Strap
Ruffle-me-Cap
Fine and Clear
Table Beer

Table beer was the weakest brew served by the Cat and Fiddle in coaching days, but the humbler inn at Ambridge, the Bull, served a less heady brew. A fragment of an old notebook which has survived with the deeds to the Bull, now in the possession of the owner, Peggy Archer, declares that two bushels of malt were expected to make

Forty gallons of Clink-me-Clear
Forty gallons of table beer
Thirty gallons of Rat-me-Tat
Fifty gallons worse than that.

One duty which the Victorian farmer's wife was not expected to perform, curiously enough, was the job of washing clothes and bedding. Teams of professional washerwomen used to tour the area visiting the main farms for a 'great buck wash' every ten weeks or so. These were the days when clothes were not washed in soap but 'lye' from wood ash. Although the practice was common throughout the Midland counties, it was a peculiar custom of Borsetshire washerwomen to boil clothes in water with a piece of suet before the lye was used.

The 'buck wash' took several days and followed a set routine. On the Wednesday evening the washerwomen would arrive, have a 'sup of gin' and bed themselves down in the farm kitchen. They would rise between three and four o'clock in the morning and prepare the lye tub: a tray containing wood ashes wrapped in cloth was filled with boiling water, which percolated through to the tub below. During Thursday the clothes would be boiled in the suet water, then washed through the lye water for the first time. On Friday they would be washed a second time. On Saturday they would again be washed and boiled, then left till Monday when they would be rinsed and hung out to dry.

The unremitting drudgery of daily life for the daughter of a cottager or poor tenant farmer no doubt accounts for the desperate desire of every village girl to find a husband or to be taken into service by the local gentry. Doris Archer went to work as a kitchen maid at the Manor House, Ambridge, in 1914 and was promoted to general maid two years later. Among her papers, now in the possession of her daughter Christine, is her daily work schedule which she copied out in her own hand and dated 23 September, 1916:

6am	Sweep hall. Light dining-room fire. Take hot water to bedrooms.
7am	Breakfast in kitchen.
7.30	Serve breakfast in dining-room. Remove dishes to kitchen.
8.30	Help make beds, clean wash stands, empty slops.
9.30	Tasks as given.
12.30	Dinner in kitchen.
1pm	Help serve dinner in dining-room. remove dishes to kitchen.
2pm	Change into afternoon dress. Tasks as given, silver cleaning, etc.
4pm	Serve tea in dining-room. Remove tea things to kitchen.
4.45	Tea in kitchen.
5pm	Turn down beds, draw bedroom blinds, light lamps.
7pm	Supper.
7.30	Wait at table only when Sally has served breakfast.
8.30	Help remove supper things to kitchen.
9pm	Take hot water to bedrooms.

It was a long day, but at no time was the pressure of work great. There was time to chat and to gossip, and as far as Doris Archer was concerned it was a life of luxury and ease when compared to her two years as a kitchen maid.

Life in the kitchen was much harder. You had to be up at half-past five to make sure the range was alight and start boiling up water. It was a monster was that range, a huge monster that ate up fifteen hundredweight of coal a week, and I carried most of it in, because the kitchen lad and gardener's lad had gone off with Squire Lawson-Hope to France. It was quite a new range, with ovens for baking and for roasting, and it had a big meat screen with a clockwork jack to turn the joint round – that was a wonder in the kitchen, the old girls thought it was a marvel not having to stand turning the joint. A lot of household aids were coming in round about then, though. We had a 'Grand Rapids' carpet sweeper, invented by an American, although Lettie Lawson-Hope still made us wash the carpets with borax and vinegar every six months, and sweep them thoroughly, on our hands and knees, with damp tea-leaves once a week. I had to do that when I was a general maid, but at least it was better than having to look after that monster of a range in the kitchen. I polished it every week for two years, and every week the heat burnt the polish off. First I had to rub it all over with stove polish and buff it up with a brush and felt pad, then the steel knobs had to be cleaned with brickdust. It was a terrible performance and I often used to think how easy my Mum had things arranged at home, where she cooked everything in one pot over the fire and never polished it at all. Everything went into that pot. The bit of bacon first, then the potatoes in a net, then the cabbage in another net, and sometimes a roly-poly pudding. If you put them in at the right time they came out cooked beautifully, and nobody had to worry about cleaning ranges with brickdust and Hedley's fairy soap and Zebo stove polish.

Doris Archer (or Forrest as she was then) worked as a general maid for eighteen months before her friend Sally Blower left to work in the Felpersham munitions factory and Doris was promoted again, to become Lettie Lawson-Hope's personal maid. Five years later she married Dan Archer, who had been given the tenancy of Brookfield Farm by the squire.

In her youth, Doris belonged to an ordered rural society that had hardly changed in five centuries. As the wife of a small tenant farmer in 1921 she milked the cows by hand, made the butter, baked in the old

River Am and Grange Farm.

bread oven, salted the pig in the autumn, fed the calves and hens and trimmed the oil lamp in the farm kitchen of an evening. During her life at Brookfield, however, she witnessed the most dramatic change in the condition of country people ever, greater even than the effect of the Black Death six centuries before or the agrarian revolution of the Georgian Age. By the time she and her husband Dan retired to Glebe Cottage (which had been left to her by Lettie Lawson-Hope), the farm was mechanized, intensively cultivated and owned by the Archer family. Sixty cows were milked each day instead of four, and the milk was taken away from the electrically-cooled vat by bulk tanker. Dan Archer was chairman of the parish council and prominent in the National Farmers' Union. Their grandson David was at public school. In the kitchen at Brookfield the oil lamps had been replaced by electricity, the salted pig that used to hang from the rafter was now unsalted, wrapped in polythene and deep-frozen. The kitchen range was enamelled, with a stainless steel towel rail, and heated at the turn of a knob from a six hundred gallon oil tank. The days of Zebo stove polish and brickdust were gone for ever.

26

Ambridge Recipes

Two local recipe books exist from the nineteenth century, one the amazing *Dinners and Ball Suppers for a Borsetshire Hunting Man by Major H—* published in 1886 and the other a splendid collection of handwritten recipes by Mrs Joan Palmer, the housekeeper to the Vicar of Ambridge between 1861 and 1894.

Before Victorian times recipes were, for most village folk, largely irrelevant. The cooking range was unknown. The cottager lived, when he was fortunate, on bread, bacon and beer, a diet of terrible monotony. Only his forced consumption of nettle soup and field vegetables in times of poverty can have saved him from a massive vitamin deficiency. The eighteenth-century squire had his roast meat and mutton pies, his game in winter, his bream or roach boiled in ale, his fruit from the garden and his classic English boiled puddings. Both sections of the community ate quantities of cheese; neither were concerned with cookery as an art.

By Mrs Palmer's day, however, the cooking range had spread into many a parsonage, and solid, middle-class, *heavy* cooking with its emphasis on vast joints of beef in rich sauces and suet-based puddings was universally popular. Some of Mrs Palmer's recipes were clearly written down from published books, but others are marked 'my own method' and one of the most delicious of these is duck with cucumber:

Chop four large cucumbers into large pieces and marinade in mild vinegar together with two chopped onions. Dredge the duck with seasoned flour. Place in stew pan with butter and brown gently on stove until all sides brown and crisp. When duck is half cooked pour off excess fat. Add half pint of good stock together with diced carrot, salt, pepper and a quarter pint of red wine. Cover the duck and let it simmer till tender. Drain cucumbers and onions and pat dry, then fry gently in fat from the duck. (Note, they will take nearly as long as the duck takes.) Add to the duck stock just before serving.

Venison was obviously a popular dish at the parsonage. Mrs Palmer's book includes four sauces; cherry, currant, orange and mulled wine. In fact Mrs Palmer used wine in her cooking to an astonishing degree, obviously respecting the taste of the Vicar (the Reverend R. G. Car-

The eighteenth-century farm.

penter, chiefly remembered now as the man who paid for the raised flagstone footpath which runs between the church and the bridge and was provided 'to save ladies' dresses and shoes being dirtied on their way to Divine Service'). At the end of her collection of recipes Mrs Palmer includes 'Borsetshire Rare-bit' – the ingredients for which she customarily left by the fire in the Vicar's sitting room, so that he could prepare his own supper after Evensong on Sunday.

Toast a slice of bread brown on both sides, then lay it in a plate before the fire. Pour a glass of claret over it and let it soak the wine up. Then cut slices of thin cheese and lay thick over the bread. Put in tin oven before the fire until toasted and browned.

But the Reverend Carpenter did not always dine on duck, venison, and toast soaked in claret – at least if the story of Joe Grundy's grandfather and the sheep's head is to be believed.

He was a bit of a rascal was my grandfather – fond of the girls, and they were fond of him. A real Grundy. Anyway, he was chasing after this kitchen maid at the vicarage, one of the Tardebigge lasses from Edgeley, and as daft as a brush. One evening he went round and there she was in the kitchen, watching over a great pot with a sheep's head and four dumplings in it. Well, my grandfather was feeling terrible hungry – they were hard times for poor tenant farmers in them days, near as bad as they are now – so he said to the Tardebigge girl, 'Why don't we play at hide-and-seek?' and she was so mooney about him she ran off and hid herself, and he grabbed himself a dumpling and ate it before taking the trouble to find her. Three times it happened, and he was just dipping in the pot for the last dumpling when he heard the vicar's pony and trap outside, so he gave the sheep's head a swirl with his long spoon and off he ran. The Tardebigge girl came back, found he was gone and looked in the pot. 'Lord help us,' she screamed. 'The sheep's head's eaten three dumplings and it's chasing round after the other one!'

The harvest was gathered loosely from the field and taken to the rick in a harvest wagon.

The Am and Lyttleton Bridge.

Mrs Palmer's book contains a recipe for boiled lamb's head which she served with the tongue and fry as a garnish, and it also has her own recipe for suet dumplings and a note reminding her to 'add chopped fried onion, bacon or parsley when making for soup'. Her basic dumpling recipe was:

Equal quantities chopped suet and flour, salt and pepper, mix with egg beaten in milk, then roll into small balls with floury hands. Drop immediately into stock or soup. Leave covered for some time to prevent heaviness.

Most of Mrs Palmer's puddings are based on rich suet pastry and the book includes the popular Victorian Kassel and Albert puddings, as well as traditional English steamed fruit and jam puddings. An interesting recipe, however, is for her own orange pudding.

Butter basin and line with suet pastry. Prick scrubbed orange all over with needle and place in centre of crust. Cover with much brown sugar and some candied orange peel. Fold over suet crust to cover, and steam for two hours. Open pastry and take out orange before serving crust steeped in orange sauce (with custard).

Beecham Bank and the 'paved way' which is now a farm track.

Mrs Palmer's recipes are now in Borchester Local History Museum (they were found among the Ambridge churchwarden's account books in 1924) and provide a fascinating, genuine insight into the food served in a Victorian parsonage. The recipe book *Dinners and Ball Suppers for a Borsetshire Hunting Man by Major H—* is something of a curiosity – a publisher's attempt to cash in on the runaway best-seller *The Pytchley Book of Refined Cookery by Major L—* which was published by Chapman and Hall and was in its fifth edition by 1886 when the Borsetshire book appeared. The recipes in *Dinners and Ball Suppers* seem slightly dated and old-fashioned – the publisher very likely used material from an earlier cookery book – but some of them are worth considering by the adventurous cook or the Borsetshire hunting man of today.

Chicken Pie

To bake a chicken pie, after you have trussed your chickens, then broken their legs and breast bones, and raised your crust of the best paste, you shall lay them in the coffin close together with their bodies full of butter: then lay upon them, and underneath them, currants, great raisins, prunes, cinnamon, sugar, whole mace and salt; then cover all with great store of butter and so bake it:

after pour into it the same liquor you did in your Marrow-bone pie, with yolks of two or three Egges beaten amongst it, and so serve forth.

Stewed Churcham Veal
Take the fillet of a cow calf, stuff it well under the udder, and at the bone and quite through to the shank. Put it into the oven with a pint of water under it, till it is a fine brown; then put it into a stew-pan, with three pints of gravy. Stew it till it is tender, and then put a few morels, truffles, a tea-spoonful of lemon pickle, a large one of browning, one of catchup, and a little cayenne pepper. Thicken it with a lump of butter rolled in flour. Take out your veal and put it into your dish, then strain the gravy, pour it over, and lay round force meat balls. Garnish with sliced lemon and pickles.

In 1949 Ambridge Women's Institute published a booklet, *Village Cookery*, which contained recipes contributed by members, and it is planned to produce an up-dated version in 1982. Below are a number of recipes from the first edition.

November Pie (Mrs Gabriel)
Cut up some leeks and clean them thoroughly before sweating them in a little butter. Line a dish with them and cover with pieces of cooked bacon. The whole mixture is topped with mashed potatoes. You can add cheese to the potato and also finish off with a layer of grated cheese before it goes into the oven to brown. (NB In place of potatoes, the pie used to be made in the village using silverweed roots, a vegetable thought to have been brought to Borsetshire by Roman Soldiers who stuffed it into their boots to stop their feet from hurting.)

Christine Archer, who was seventeen and had just left school and joined the Ministry of Agriculture as an outside milk sampler, contributed a recipe she had learned in domestic science, Half-pay pudding, a dish which goes back to the early nineteenth century.

Half-Pay Pudding (Miss C. Archer)
Bind together a quarter pound each of breadcrumbs, flour, suet, currants and raisins, with one cup of milk, one teaspoon of baking powder and two tablespoons of golden syrup. Steam this until ready. A very filling pud for a cold winter's day!

Another economical dish was contributed by Mrs Dorothy Cooper, a farmworker's wife, who was given the recipe by her own mother. Chop pies were a way of making one chop stretch round a whole family, by making up to ten pies for high tea on a Saturday.

Chop Pies (Mrs D. Cooper)
Bone a good chump chop, then chop it finely and cook it in a little butter or dripping with one tablespoon of minced onion. After they are cooked dust the fat with flour to brown and add half a pint of stock to make a good thick gravy. While it is cooling, line small patty tins with flaky pastry and fill them with the meat, onion and gravy mix. After putting a top on them, cook for up to half an hour in a hot oven.

Ridge and furrow ploughing runs down to Eadric's Ditch.

The traditional Borsetshire high tea is, of course, world famous and the WI booklet contains several of the hot meat dishes favoured for high tea in Ambridge, as well as recipes for several of the cakes that are such a speciality of the area.

Oxtail and Beans (Mrs Blossom)
Bring the pieces of oxtail to the boil in just enough water to cover them. Add ten peppercorns, one onion, three cloves, salt, chopped parsley and let simmer gently for an hour. Skim off fat and strain off gravy. Add one chopped turnip, two sliced carrots, one large onion, sliced. Pour back the stock and simmer till tender. Melt one ounce butter, stir in one desertspoonful of flour and let it colour slightly. Stir in a little of the stock and heat, stirring, until it thickens. Pour back into the pan with the meat and heat for ten minutes. Serve with a border of boiled haricot beans, and bread and butter.

Cabbage and Bacon (Mrs J. Archer)
Cut three savoys in half and boil in salted water for fifteen minutes, then put under cold water and drain well in a sieve. Line bottom of a fireproof dish with bacon and put the cabbage on top. Just cover with stock, then put another layer of bacon on top. Cover and simmer about an hour and a half, until the liquor is absorbed by the cabbage. (Note: ground cloves can be added to the salt and pepper seasoning of the cabbage if desired.)

Chocolate Potato Cake (Mrs Fairbrother)
Cream together half pound castor sugar and two and a half oz butter. Add one beaten egg and stir in five oz of hot mashed potato. Sift together six oz flour, a pinch of salt, three quarters of a level teaspoon of cinnamon, three level teaspoons of baking powder and a quarter of a grated nutmeg, and add it to the creamed mix alternately with a quarter gill of hot milk in which has been dissolved one and a half oz of chocolate and another beaten egg.

Bullocks at Home Farm.

Bake in two sandwich tins for twenty to thirty minutes and sandwich together with lemon cheese and chopped walnuts. Decorate top with vanilla flavoured icing.

Flannel Cakes (Miss Grace Fairbrother)
Sift half pound of flour with a third of a teaspoon of carbonate of soda and a quarter teaspoon of salt. Rub in a walnut of butter and add one oz of castor sugar. Put the yolks of two eggs into the flour, gradually stir in half a pint of milk and mix to a smooth batter, then add another quarter pint of milk. Stir in the stiffly whisked whites. Cook in a small frying pan in lard like pancakes. (Should be served in winter, with last year's strawberry jam.)

Borsetshire is well-known for lamb – home-grown Spring lamb from the Hassett Hills, cooked with rosemary and served with redcurrant jelly. In late spring legs of lamb decorate butchers' windows, skewered into aprons of fat (locally known as 'sold in the caul'). The fat comes from near the kidney, and as the joint is cooked the caul brings out the flavour. The real triumph of the Borsetshire kitchen, however, used to be the leg or saddle of mutton, a meat that is today virtually unobtainable. During the Second World War it was served in hotels and restaurants – but the tough, strong ewe meat obtained from old sheep that were past lambing can have born little resemblance to an eighteenth-century saddle of Hassett mutton, killed at four years old. Doris Archer used to boil half legs of mutton and serve with caper sauce.

Put half a leg of mutton (knuckle end) into boiling water with a little salt. Remove the scum and boil rapidly for few minutes to seal in the flavour, then simmer for about one and a half hours. Peel two pounds of onions, wrap them

The Bull.

in muslin, add a few turnips when in season, and boil them for about an hour along with the meat.

Serve the meat hot with the vegetables and a little of the liquid. Save the rest of the liquid for the sauce to eat with the rest of the mutton when cold. For the sauce melt one and a half oz butter in a saucepan, add three quarters of a pint meat liquid and stir until thick. Pour in the drained capers from a fourpenny ha'penny bottle, add a spoonful of vinegar from the caper bottle, stir well and serve.

Until the late fifties Doris Archer used to salt a pig every year, using the farm 'salting lead' – a large leaden trough in wooden base – that had served its purpose for upwards of a century. Until the thirties a traveller visited Ambridge twice a year selling wedge-shaped bars of Droitwich salt that had to be crushed up before use. Bacon is still salted on several farms in the Ambridge area, including Grange Farm where Joe Grundy uses the traditional method.

First you cut the pig up into flitches of bacon and hams and pack them into the salting lead with the odd bits – feet, and cheek and jowls. That's where the saying comes from, cheek by jowl. Not everybody knows that these days. Then you sprinkle salt over and rub a couple of ounces of saltpetre into the hams and thick bits of bacon to help the salt to penetrate. Anyway, you just rub salt in every other day for two or three weeks, then drain the meat and dry it and hang it up till it's ready for use.

Index